Like Myth Made Flesh
Erotic Encounters with Mythical Beings

edited by Jennifer Williams

Circlet Press, Inc.
Cambridge, MA

Contents

Introduction

Many of us dream of being something greater than what we are; something powerful, something special, maybe even something to be worshiped. We find ways, in our everyday lives, to fulfill these dreams. We cut from the fabric of the lives we are given, mold and shape the stones of our paths, to fit our desires and fantasies; for some, this means simple role playing in the privacy of our bedrooms, or, if we're braver, in a fetish club or at a party. For others, it simply means trying to be a better person, to echo the tenets of the gods we worship in the actions of our daily lives. For others still, it means calling to our gods, offering up our bodies, our wills, and our spirits in their service.

What if they answered? What if they came to us, not in dreams or in spirit, but in flesh and blood that we could feel with our skin and our teeth, and the beating of their hearts beneath our hands? How would it feel to have them wrap their arms around us and claim us as theirs? How would it change us to know that we were chosen? To be shown things that most mortals never get to see or experience?

When I put out my call for submissions for my previous Circlet anthology, *Like a Sacred Desire: Tales of Sex Magick*, this fantasy came to the forefront of the minds of the authors who submitted their work. There were Egyptian gods, Aztec gods, nymphs, and various other magical creatures. I decided that these stories needed their own separate anthology where they could shine on their own, not unlike a candle upon the altar of a dimly lit room. *Like a Sacred Desire: Tales of Sex Magick* was the incantation. It was the drawing down of the moon, the offering we made of ourselves, and this collection is the answer, the fruit of those labors in which the gods make themselves known.

The stories contained herein are not all easy reads. There is pain, fear, and loss, but there is also hope and redemption and devotion. The characters you will meet are all on varied paths. Some are struggling with regret. Some have souls that have dried up, stifling their creativity. Others are just beginning their spiritual journeys, and yet others are faced with choices that could change them forever.

As you'll see in this collection, the divine does not exist solely outside of us. It resides within us also, a well waiting to be tapped. These stories ask you to face your fears, to embrace the sacred within you, and ultimately to be true to yourself and who you are meant to be. The passion, strength, and wisdom lie within you whether you believe in one god or in many. It is with you always, in every little thing you do, from giving thanks for a meal to appreciating the bright sun and the silver moon as they travel across the sky from day to day. You have only to listen, to hear the whispers of the divine in each step of your day. Maybe, just maybe, if you believe in them they will believe in you.

With Faith and Blessings,

Jennifer Williams
November 2016

Initiation
Christina M. Parker

They call me Tezcatlipoca. Smoking Mirror. The name tells only part of the story for I am the Spirit Mirror as well. I reflect Truth. The truth of self that burns the soul. The weak fear me for they only see my power to consume and destroy. Those who are strong, who can withstand the heat of my gaze, who willingly give themselves over to my power, have no need to fear for they are my beloved ones. I burn for my beloveds as they burn for me and it is within that embrace that my real power lies...

Flirting with danger, no, that didn't describe me that night. A lone woman, walking the streets of Mexico City during the height of the Dias de los Muertos—the Mexican Days of the Dead—is not flirting with danger. I was screaming for it to come and find me. I think the part of me that would have stopped me from doing so was too shocked to act. It would not have made any difference, though. I know that now. I knew it at the time. The place, the setting, my actions were exactly what they needed to be. I did not know why. Entranced by a craving for something I could not name, I did not have to know why.

From the corner of my eye, I caught a glimpse of a woman watching the procession from the safety of her doorway. Our eyes met and, for a brief instant, I was staring at an image of myself. A trick of the eye or the mind, perhaps, but I knew I was looking at the past. The image I saw no longer existed. I had stepped across some imaginary threshold and left the self-imposed prison I had built with my illusions of safety and security. Meeting my responsibilities, maintaining a sense of security, struggling to find that middle ground that tells the world that I'm "normal"—those were the activities that absorbed my time and energy within that prison. Whenever ideas of adventure or romance would slip past the carefully erected barriers in my mind, I turned to books to fulfill those fantasies. Other people, real or imagined, could make great achievements. They had the internal strength to weather the highs and lows that accompanied taking emotional and physical risks. Not me, I held fast to the three R's drilled into me since childhood—reason, responsibility, and restraint.

I did not falter in my determined pace as I passed the woman. Although acutely focused on my objective, a small part of my mind mused on the chain of events that drew me across the vast chasm now separating me from my carefully constructed shelters.

I'd been intrigued rather than concerned by the fascination I had when I first learned about the Dias de los Muertos. At first I kept my interest to scholarly investigations. I researched the various spiritual beliefs and how the festival activities vary depending upon where they are held. However, nothing I did satisfied my interest. In fact, the more I learned, the more I became convinced that there was something specific in it for me. For whatever reason, I needed to actually go and experience the festival in person.

That's when my detached interest turned into palpable fear. I would be alone in a foreign country with limited ability to communicate due to a lack of understanding both the language and the customs of the people around me. It was too risky—too outrageously irresponsible, in my opinion, for a small woman inexperienced with foreign travel to even consider. However, I continued my research and found a guided tour specifically designed to allow people the experience of Dias de los Muertos in Mexico City while providing the safety of numbers and knowledgeable guides. So, I booked my spot on the tour, went through the bureaucratic process of getting my first passport, and eagerly awaited my vacation. Three months later, as I settled into my hotel room, I congratulated myself for being clever enough to find a way to complete my quest and pursue the adventure I assumed awaited me that night. It never entered my mind that my quest had not even begun.

So naïve. Ignorant fragility is dust in my mouth. I can erase the illusion of security as easily as you can breathe. Naïve, but willing. It is the willingness that stayed my hand. It is faint, true. But still strong enough for me to taste and whet my appetite for more.

I thought my research had prepared me, but nothing except experience could have prepared me for the sights, sounds, and smells that brutally assaulted my senses the moment I stepped outside of the hotel—and hiding in my sheltered, closed-in little life back in New England gave me no such experience to draw upon for the comfort of familiarity. In my world, death masqueraded as a tall, thin man of solemn expression, it crept silently in small, shuttered rooms, cloaked in shades of black and grey, it smelled of old roses and camphor, and its raspy breath spoke only in whispers or softly chanted dirges. Here, a lusty woman served as Death's avatar. It invaded the streets, proudly marching in parades, leaving whirlpools of dancers celebrating with wild abandon in its wake. It came gaily, even garishly, dressed in vibrant reds, oranges, and yellows with flowers adorning its smiling skulls. It reeked with the aromas of unwashed bodies, cinnamon, rotting fruit, grilled meats, and spicy peppers. Death allowed no dirges in its revelries; steel drums, African drums, guitars, trumpets, castanets, maracas, and human voices all competed to be the loudest in singing praises to La Muerte. I'd seen pictures and read descriptions, but they all fell far short of reality.

In hindsight, I think the main reason my research failed me was the energy pulsing through the air of the city. Every place has its own special energy, it changes slightly with time of day and season of the year—like variations on the same musical theme—and it's just not possible to feel energy from a book. I'd felt the alien difference when I left the airport that morning, but it quickly became a background hum once my other senses became engaged by the unfamiliar surroundings. I didn't know nights during Dias de los Muertos brought a dramatic transformation to the city—and thus to its energy.

Standing in the street, it didn't matter that I was surrounded by the other tourists in my group—and under the watchful eye of our guide—the energy still found me and hit me with a physical impact. It wrapped around me and then drilled into the core of my being. Primal, fearless, aggressive, beautiful, grieving, exhilarating, I felt all of it and more. I felt things that cannot be described within the pages of an entire book, yet those who share the experience can summon and recall those feelings by a mere glance and nod at each other. In another time and place, I probably would have shut down due to sensory overload (one of the reasons I avoided crowds), but that night I kept inviting more and basking in whatever came my way.

My head bobbed back and forth like a spectator at tennis match at first and then I began to turn with my whole body in order to better bathe in the spectacle. As I made my third or fourth full turn, just out of the corner of my eye, I caught sight of a pair of golden eyes peering out of a void, and they captured my attention like nothing else in that sea of chaos. When I shifted back to get a clear view, I couldn't find them. It wasn't just that the eyes were lost in the visual spectacle surrounding me, the void was gone too. I couldn't see it, but I knew it was still there. My heart hammered as a sense of panic filled me. I didn't fear the crowds, the eyes and the void were all that mattered now, and I was scared I wouldn't find them again. They were all I could feel. When I stopped my turnings and paused to take a breath, a faint drumbeat made itself known to me through everything else clamoring for my attention and I had to follow the sound. It was calling to me.

When I say that I had to follow the sound, I do not mean to imply that I did not have a choice. I was in complete control of my actions. There was no reason why I couldn't stay with the tour group. The call was an invitation, not a spell of compulsion. However, I did not think twice about accepting the invitation. I did not know what was being offered, but I felt the sacredness of the offering. Safety or sacrilege—the choice that really wasn't a choice since I held only one option in my heart. So, while the tour group headed one way, I went the other.

At first I was led directly into the heart of the festivities. A small person in a large crowd, I was defenseless against the crush of bodies that did not appear to have any clear direction to their movements. If there was a direction, I was moving against it. Under normal circumstances, I would have been overwhelmed with panic. Instead, I felt the strength and power that comes with the conviction that one is under Divine protection. I used my size to my advantage as I wiggled and squirmed into whatever small openings presented themselves in the crowd. At one point, the noise from the crowd drowned out the drums and the panic I felt earlier when I lost sight of the eyes and the void threatened to return. Surprisingly, when I fought to calm myself so I could find the sound again, the eyes and the void appeared again just on the edge of my vision. As before, they were gone when I turned to look at them, but the sound of the drums returned to lead me further on the trail.

I do not know how far I walked or exactly where I went that night. Through crowds, down deserted side streets, at one point the drums even led me in one door and out the other of a hotel. I may have walked a straight line or circled back many times before I reached my destination. I had no direction or landmarks except for the sound of the drums. Yes, I felt powerful and strong, but I also felt vulnerable. I felt the danger in the crowds and in the dark, isolated areas even as I was guided through them. For once in my life I did not let my vulnerability deter me. I embraced it and it fed me. As I said in the beginning, I was not flirting with danger, I was screaming for it. I could feel it in the energy around me and in the beat of the drums. As I walked, I realized that my thoughts had dwindled to a single mantra set to the rhythm of the drums— feed me, fill me, everything, all.

Ah, the memory of that sweet elixir of willingness still lingers. The ignorance has vanished. You feel my power and hear my call. It pleases me, but I am not satisfied yet. You hear, it is true, but you do not understand.

I stood in front of an open doorway. I could not see what lay within, but I knew my destination (and maybe my destiny) was on the other side. I had caught sight of the eyes in the doorway as I turned the corner onto the street. The sound of the drums surrounded me. I had already stepped across a spiritual threshold, now all that remained was for me to cross this physical one. So I did.

The room was dim. Thinking back, I don't know what provided the light in the room. I could feel a sense of enclosure but the darkness beyond the light was so complete that the walls and ceiling were not visible. There were three drummers in the center of the light but when I stepped into circle, they silently picked up their instruments and retreated to the darkness. Other than their exit, they did not acknowledge my presence.

I stood in silence. After being inundated with the sounds from the festival and the drums, the silence assaulted my senses and I felt disoriented by it. However, without the sounds and sights overwhelming them, my other senses reemerged. I felt a presence in the darkness. It was circling me, examining me, challenging me. My spirit answered in the only way left to it now——feed me, fill me, everything, all.

I saw the eyes first, but the form attached to them emerged

almost simultaneously from the dark void. In answering the invitation, I sought danger and I found it in a way I would never have imagined. I was alone in a room with a jaguar. Oh yes, danger with a capital J. Instead of fear, however, I felt exhilaration. The jaguar roared in satisfaction at my reaction—and my recognition. My research finally served a purpose because I knew the jaguar for what it was—a manifestation of the Aztec god Tezcatlipoca.

I knew that this was a threat far beyond anything a mere animal could pose and my reaction to that knowledge surprised me as much as anything else that I'd experienced so far that night. Until that moment, I was oblivious to the emotions that were the real source of my feelings of vulnerability. I had become so out of touch with my own sexuality that I did not recognize the energy that coursed through me since I stepped outside of my hotel. With each step I'd taken, the tension inside me had increased until the presence of Tezcatlipoca pushed me to the verge of an orgasm and forced me to acknowledge my long-suppressed sexual needs.

True, your awareness pleased me. One more layer lifted, but so many more to remove before you will understand. Willing vulnerability, so few have the strength to face that fire. To understand its secrets, you must let it burn within you.

How do you seduce a God? I had never really thought about that question because it did not occur to me that I might have occasion to want to do so. Thankfully, I did not stop to ponder the question. For once the part of my brain that loves to analyze every nuance of questions like that was silent. "Strip," said an authoritative voice in my head, so I obeyed.

I am usually self-conscious about my body and seek to hide those less-than-perfect parts when I undress in front of someone. Under other circumstances, feeling the cool gaze of someone as I stood naked in front of them would be an emotional ordeal. These were not normal circumstances and I was not standing in front of "someone." I was more naked in front of Tezcatlipoca while I wore clothes. Not only was there no point in trying to hide from his gaze, I did not even want to try. I yearned for the freedom of knowing that I had nothing left hidden from him. I stripped without fanfare or show, but with a simple grace and elegance I did not know I possessed.

I'm certain that his eyes never left me as he slowly paced a circle around me while I stripped. There were times when I couldn't see it, but never a time when I didn't feel it. I stood there in the light for minutes or hours, time didn't matter. As long as he wished it, I would have stayed there. I still felt the vulnerability. In fact, the feeling grew stronger as his gaze continued to bore into me. Yet my vulnerability carried the power and beauty of the moment and I embraced all of it equally. Neither of us was satisfied; we were both hungry for more. "Lie down," said the same authoritative voice I had heard earlier, which I now knew for certain to be him, and I did.

Still testing my resolve, he used his paws to nudge my legs apart. I don't know if it was a response of challenge or cooperation, but there was no need for him to do more than slightly nudge my legs because as soon as he did I spread them wide in invitation. Whether it was a sign of pleasure or issuing a further challenge, his roar when my legs parted sent a jolt of energy that bounced from my clitoris up into my womb. He stepped across me and straddled my body. He remained standing in that position, but I still felt enveloped by him. I could feel the heat of his body as it covered mine and the light caress of his tail as it swung casually back and forth between my legs. I smelled his musky scent and felt his breath on my face as he gazed down into my eyes.

As I returned his stare, I saw that the void did not surround his eyes, it resided within them. Far from wanting to look away, I wanted to lose myself in his gaze. Feed me, fill me, everything, all.

That wasn't enough. I needed to dig deeper and go farther than I had ever gone. The void was not a void, it was dark power. It was my dark power. This was not evil, this was Divine. I felt my darkness in all its glorious beauty—healing, cleansing, creating— definitely dangerous, potentially destructive, but necessary. The power of it flooded me and I roared as I lifted my arms to embrace the One who had released it.

When I lifted my arms, he lowered his head and I could feel his teeth sink into my neck. Well, it was my neck but it wasn't my neck. I didn't have my arms around him, they were my paws and my claws were digging into his back. The sexual component that had been hovering around the energy between us burst into center stage as the reality of my physical transformation dawned on me. Raw, primal, animal instinct reigned. And not just any animal, I was a jaguar—pure feline power in all its magnificent glory. I now had the physical ability to accept his passion and match it with my own. Biting, clawing, grappling, rolling over each other— sometimes sideways, sometimes end over end—we did anything and everything to get more of each other. I forgot we were human and deity and lost myself to the frenzy of a female jaguar in heat.

I may have forgotten, but he never did. He was in position to mount me. If my sounds had been in human voice, the words would have been alternating between begging and challenging him to take me. It happened so quickly I don't even know how I changed positions. I was still under him, but now I was face up. Instead of being held captive by his body, I was once again enthralled by his gaze. It took me a moment to comprehend that I was human again because I did not lose any of the power I was feeling when the physical transformation occurred. In fact, it was the slight change in energy that brought my awareness back. There was something new, something different in the energy between us, and I plumbed the depths of his gaze in an attempt to identify the new element.

I reached for the reflection of dark power that I last found in his eyes. It was there, but the void was there as well. The void was not a reflection. It was not mine; I was overflowing. He had given me the strength to release the darkness and fill the void within me. The void I saw this time was his. I had been begging and challenging him to take me, now he was telling me that if I wanted him to take me then I had to accept him as well. For the first time in his presence, I felt fear. I did not fear him; I feared for him. I feared the limitations of my abilities. If I accepted him, I had to accept the responsibility of his trust. Could I meet that responsibility?

Why should I fear for him? He is a god and I am a mortal. He is not just any god; he is the most powerful and dangerous of all the Aztec gods. As an ordinary human, I did not possess the power to harm him. As a woman in his arms, however, he was offering me that power. He was offering to lay himself bare before me as I had done for him. He had my passion but he needed my love. That was the void I saw inside him. Did I have the strength to fill it? The answer swirled around me and through me and I rejoiced in the power of it. Yes. Feed me, fill me, everything, all.

Afraid for me? You still did not understand the lesson. Embrace what you have learned, embrace me, and I will show you. Will you see it then?

This time when I raised my arms to embrace him and he bent down to bite my neck, it was my arms that encircled him and a man's teeth that grazed my skin. We had shared our passion as felines, but I needed my true form in order to accept everything he needed to give me. With his teeth on my neck, I felt his power to destroy was just as strong in his human form as it was in his jaguar manifestation. However, those teeth did not sink into my flesh; the light graze and brief nip at my exposed jugular vein demonstrated his control over that power. I stroked the muscles of his back with my palms and felt his restraint in the tension of his muscles.

He wanted me to feel the tenderness of his healing touch and I melted in bliss as he gently caressed me. A soft stroke on my cheek, cupping my breast in his hand and lazily rolling my hard nipple between his thumb and finger, reaching underneath and kneading the muscles of my buttocks, easing apart my labia and teasing me with a swift kiss on my clit, he showed me in so many ways the joy he takes in the beauty of his creations. I had to fight my instincts to stop him when he began to massage my feet. He is a god, I should be at his feet—but he is a god and, therefore, he should be wherever he chooses to be.

He moved to lay beside me and when he kissed me I still felt his restraint but it was much thinner. When he put his fingers inside me and began rubbing my clit with his thumb, the intense pleasure pushed all remaining worries from my mind. He was inside me and I could feel his energy coursing through me. Yet it still wasn't enough. The more I got, the more I wanted. I thrilled to the knowledge of his willingness to give more when he guided my head towards his cock.

Sucking the cock of a god is tasting the pure essence of Divine masculine energy——not just tasting it, but smelling it, feeling it, hearing its pulse, seeing it in a way that you could never imagine and cannot describe. I had his cock in my mouth but I was totally enveloped by him. I could have stayed there for hours and each second would have brought a new sensation and experience. I barely had time to adjust to the shock of just holding him in my mouth when he began fucking it. Dangerous, glorious, beautiful, dark, primal power radiated from us both. I didn't worry about whether I could physically take it—I had his power coursing through my soul. I could do anything.

He stopped fucking my mouth as abruptly as he had started. He did not allow me any time to register the loss, however, as he quickly pulled me up and under him. Although by now I had been subjected to the weight of his gaze numerous times, I still felt the power and the danger within it. Only an ignorant fool would take such a thing lightly. The dark power flowed from its depths, yet the void was still there. It was so small that it could have gone unnoticed, but not by me. It called to me with an intensity that burned. The question was there again, but there was no doubt about the answer. Feed me, fill me, everything, all.

As he plunged his cock deep within me, my body responded by exploding in orgasm. This was merely the beginning, however. Each thrust brought new waves of sensation. Pain, pleasure, pride, isolation, triumph, grief, compassion, shame, forgiveness, respect, decadence, chaos, horror, he held nothing back. Everything he is he showed me and I accepted it all. I didn't just see it, I felt it. I let it all pour into me. I drank his essence and let it blend with my own. When I felt his body climax and the last remnants burst into me, I let go of everything and fed it back to him through the power of my answering orgasm. I fed it back so he could feel my love wrapped around every part of it.

Gasping for breath in the aftermath, I kept my head turned to the side as I lay underneath him. For the first time, I feared his gaze. Relief mixed with triumphant power when my courage allowed me to risk it. The void was gone.

I had been stretched to the limits of my emotional, spiritual, and physical endurance. It was no wonder that I fell asleep within minutes as he held me close. When I awoke, he was gone. I had expected that. I was surprised to see the three drummers silently standing guard over me. I was also touched that they respected my modesty by standing with their backs to me. As I dressed, I wondered how I would find my way back to my hotel. It crossed my mind that I might have passed into another world and there would be no going back to my hotel—or to my home. Part of me even hoped for that to be true. My experience had changed me in ways I couldn't even identify yet. Even if it were physically possible, could I ever really go back?

I could, and I did. My guards kept their silence, but they communicated clearly without words. They escorted me back to the hotel as dawn crept across the streets of Mexico City. When we reached the front door of the hotel, I thanked them for their help.

They bowed and left. I did not look back to see which direction they took—they had respected my privacy while I slept and I sensed that they wished for me to do the same for them.

I am home now as I write this. Any experience can change you if you let it, and mine was no different. I don't know yet what direction those changes will lead me to take, but I cannot go on as if nothing ever happened. Even if I wanted to try and convince myself that I imagined the whole thing, the scars of the wound inflicted by the jaguar's claws are very real. He only marked me in one place, but the white ridges on the skin over my heart were all that was necessary to make the point.

Did you understand the lesson? Do you sense the secret? The power is yours to claim. Can you find the path that will lead you to me? Search your fears and hear my call. Leave the deadly stillness of your prisons and embrace life as my beloveds do.

Sun Chases Moon
Michael M. Jones

Tonight, I kissed the Moon.

For the longest time, I knew Phoebe Masters only as this sly-smiling, silver-haired, sapphire-eyed enigma who ran in the same circles I did, our paths intersecting time and again with minimal interaction. We orbited one another, gazes meeting at events and occasions, exchanging nods and smiles. All the while, a slow burning desire far outstripped my understanding of her.

I first saw her at Bifrost Books, when we both turned up to meet Katie Carruthers, a local author who'd achieved prominence for her emotionally raw, tightly-plotted mysteries about a lesbian cop, set right here in Puxhill. Her books had given me strength and hope when I needed them most; this was my chance to say thank you. Phoebe was several places ahead of me in line, close enough for me to admire the way she filled out her tank top and jeans, and imagine stroking the pale skin of her exposed arms. Perhaps sensing my interest, she turned, catching me before I could look away and pretend I'd been studying something innocuous. There was no accusation or offense in her expression, just an enigmatic smile. She held the meeting of eyes long enough for me to know it was deliberate, reading me in my moment of awkward exposure. Her lips twitched, and that was it. She turned as the line moved forward by another person, leaving me to wonder just what had happened, and what I'd missed. When she got to Katie, they exchanged words, too quiet for me to catch. Katie blushed, Phoebe laughed, and when the signing was over, they left the store together, arm in arm. I went home with nothing but my personalized books for company; though I'd long crushed on Katie for her writing, it was Phoebe who invaded my fantasies that night, who touched and stroked and licked me until I came with surprising intensity. I was still lost in that unrealized moment of connection in the bookstore, drawn to her eyes, and it... unsettled me.

I thought about it the next day at work, my body on autopilot while my mind raced. It wasn't the first time I'd fallen in lust at a glance; my dating history was littered with rash decisions and snap judgments. I'd run both towards and away from women ever since my last year of high school, when a drunken hook-up at the after-prom party led to selective amnesia for my best friend and a lifestyle choice for me. But there's a difference between attraction and a magnetic pull; every time I lost focus, my brain boomeranged right on back to the issue of Phoebe.

The moon rose and fell, waxed and waned, and Phoebe's intrusions into my life were as regular as the tides. I saw her at the Blackbird Café, where she charmed the waitress away from my table before I could work up the courage to ask either of them out. Phoebe was there at Club Armageddon, dancing up a storm in tight leather pants and a low-cut corset which exposed far too much of her cleavage for my peace of mind. Tall and slender, she was curvy in all the ways I could appreciate; by the time she vanished with the heavily-pierced and tattooed drummer from Hedgehog Apocalypse, I was wet from watching her move, and not a step closer to figuring things out.

When I next saw her, at a bout between the Caravan Street Hussies and the Tuesday University Trollops to determine the champions of the Puxhill Rollergirl League, I cornered her. "Why not me?" I asked, as bold and brazen as you please, meeting her eyes to hold her attention. Until that moment, I hadn't known what I'd say. The words exploded from my lips, gaining unexpected freedom. It reminded me of the freedom I'd felt as a blocker for the Trollops, until one knee injury too many took me out of the game for good. I never missed a bout if I could help it, regardless.

Her smile was slow and knowing. "Because the Sun must always chase the Moon, Malina." That night, she chose a purple-haired jammer from the Hussies, while I went home alone, rather than pursue someone who wasn't Phoebe. She knew my name. I wasn't some faceless stranger to her, some anonymous bystander. She knew me. We went to the same places, we knew the same people, and we had the same taste in bed partners, except that I dreamed of her silver hair falling over my breasts, her slim fingers touching me, her tongue teasing around my nipples. I'd no idea if she found me, a short, stocky Spanish-Hawaiian-Swedish mutt without a trace of elegance in her body, attractive at all. I came to thoughts of her, yearning fingers buried in my pussy, while outside the full moon hung in a cloudless sky, my window open to call in the night air.

The moon rose and fell, waxed and waned, and I grew no closer to unraveling what attracted me to Phoebe, yet repelled her from me. During the day, as I fulfilled orders for bouquets and floral arrangements at Riotous Bloom Florists, I dreamed of her dropping in to see me. While the dreams were occasionally as vivid as real life, she never did. She had no use for flowers, not when all she needed to win over a woman was a sly smile, a throaty laugh, and a crook of the finger. Not when she remained an unattainable mystery. Several times, I tracked down her conquests, for questioning, only to learn they knew as little as I did. A fantastic lover, an enthusiastic partner, an unforgettable experience... and not a one could tell me anything of her private life, of likes or dislikes, hobbies or interests, friends or family. She was a mystery, slipping between their mental fingers like quicksilver. I found out that she was a DJ, hosting a late night show on the local classical station. I left it on at night, falling asleep to her voice as she introduced me to Mozart and Haydn, Holst and Strauss. My dreams were full of silver.

I never saw her in the daytime.

I presented myself to her again, this time at the Friday Movie in Morrison Park, where a crowd had gathered to lounge on the grass, eat barbeque and take-out, and watch Pretty In Pink on the big screen. Phoebe was there alone—but not for long, I knew—and I sat myself down next to her. "Why not me?" I asked again, skipping right over the intervening months. I'd practiced a dozen speeches and a hundred come-ons, rehearsed the moment countless times, and the second I was face-to-face with her, it all fell away again.

This time, she reached out, one purple-nailed hand perching on my jeans-clad thigh. "I told you. The Sun must always chase the Moon." The touch short-circuited my thoughts, and I wasted precious seconds recapturing them, trying to decipher what I read in her solemn eyes. Her succinctness spoke volumes of significance, calling to something deep within me.

I clearly took too long, for her expression grew distant again, even disappointed. Just then, I frantically grasped at one forgotten snippet before it, and the moment, were lost. "The Moon also chases the Sun!" I blurted out.

Phoebe chuckled, withdrawing her hand and rising to her feet in one smooth motion. "True. And sometimes, one catches the other." Her gaze flicked upwards to a clear, starry sky, then back to me. "But not often, and not tonight." Her fingers just barely brushed my hair, a gesture somewhere between taunting and affectionate. She walked away while I was still tingling from the charge she'd sent through me. My nipples were tight with arousal, my panties damp, just from being near her, from the way her words wrapped around me, and it was several moments before I could think to move again. By that time, Phoebe had chosen a bi-curious soccer mom who'd only recently come out of the closet, and that was that.

The moon rose and fell, waxed and waned, and I did my homework. Instinctively, I knew Phoebe had already given me everything I needed to solve her mystery. She wanted me to chase her. She wanted my persistence, but for me to claim the reward, I had to understand the when, where, and why. The pattern wasn't in her choices; she'd shown no particular preference for looks or temperament, age or occupation. She'd walked away with femme and butch, athletes and scholars. But only once a month. I'd never seen her choose someone more often than that, and of course, never the same one twice. And never me.

I watched and waited, putting together the clues. I touched myself at night, eyes shut so I could pretend it was Phoebe's tongue on my clit, her nails raking my skin. I'd never gone this long without a girlfriend or fuckbuddy, but as long as I pursued Phoebe, that didn't matter. They weren't her, and it wouldn't be right to pretend otherwise. I killed several vibrators in the meantime, and slept with the window open as much as possible, inviting in the night air and the moonlight. Each morning, I woke refreshed, but unsatisfied, the yearning returning as the day passed. Roses and carnations, daisies and lilies and sunflowers passed through my hands, destined for friends and family, lovers and mourners, and all the while, I waited for the right moment.

Tonight, it all came together. For once, I knew exactly where to find her. Shortly before sunset, I made my way to Morrison Park, though this time it wasn't to catch a movie. I settled in with my iPod, letting Audra Hardt and Marion Raven bolster my courage, while all around, people gathered, arriving in trickles and groups, bringing a festive atmosphere with them. Night fell in force, and the full moon slowly rose over the city, brilliant and sharp against the sky. It was close to midnight before, Phoebe settled in next to me, taking up a cross-legged position, purple broomstick skirt falling over her lap. I removed my earbuds, turning to look at her, and was rewarded with a proud smile, her pale lips curving up in sensuous approval. "You know," she said.

"I'm pretty sure," I replied. I offered my right hand to her, palm up, and she delicately laid her fingers in mine. I was prepared for the shock of contact, but even so, the buzz leaping through me was more invigorating than anything I'd imagined. I gasped sharply, even as my toes curled. Her skin hummed.

"Sun chases Moon," Phoebe said. "Moon chases Sun. Every once in a while, they catch each other. But not often. When it happens, it's memorable, and spectacular."

"A lunar eclipse on the second full moon in a month—a blue moon. That's got to be pretty damned memorable," I said. She nodded, simply. "Who *are* you?" I asked, studying her intently. She was always beautiful, with fine features and oh-so-kissable lips and those knowing sapphire eyes, but tonight she was radiant. Her skin glowed, and her hair tumbled down around her shoulders to frame her face, rounding the sharper edges and softening the overall effect. She wore a cream-colored blouse that gaped at the neckline, granting me a glimpse of cleavage, more than hinting at her small, tight breasts. Though a night chill had fallen, she paid it no heed.

She studied me back, long enough for me to wonder if she planned to reply. I wondered what she thought. Whether she approved. I'd worn my favorite jeans, and a tight emerald shirt that had served me well in the past. I knew the combination, while simple, showed off my own ample curves quite nicely, and the color went well against my dark skin, eyes and hair. Finally, she smiled again. "There's a question open to interpretation. Mostly? I'm Phoebe Masters. I live alone with one cat and a cactus, I work nights and sleep days, and I'm very good at computer solitaire. That's enough for most people."

I listened to her simple recitation of the bare facts of her existence. It sounded so... empty. "You're so much more than that," I said.

Her shoulders rose and fell. "I suppose I am. You're not most people. Of course that's not enough for you. Who do you think I am?"

It was my turn to take my time answering. Truth be told, I'd never felt anything quite as nice as sitting in the park, in the dark, with Phoebe's hand in mine, and I was reluctant to move past the moment. But then, I found the words. "You're a goddess, aren't you?"

"I am." For a second, I thought that's all the answer I'd get. The questions bubbled at my lips, but she continued, voice hinting at something both wry and tragic. "I am Moon. I've had a hundred different names and origins, but none are completely correct, just as no one story defines me. Some come closer than others, but for every one that's survived in stories and fragmented texts, there's a dozen others lost to history because no one thought to record it."

Her fingers intertwined in mine. I scooted closer, until we were resting against one another under the full moon. She laid her head on my shoulder, still speaking in her low, rhythmic manner. "I am Moon, and I am eternal. I live and die as the world turns, and yet I persist. People explain me, and define me, but they don't know me."

There was something old and painfully lonely in her tone, the sensation of falling through endless vacuum with none to catch you, and I shivered. "Why are you telling me this?" I asked.

"Why not? You won't remember come the morning. No one ever does," she said with a bitter laugh. "Catch me, love me for a night, wake as if from a dream. You're satisfied, I'm renewed for another month, the cycle continues."

Around us, people gasped, pointing up at the sky, where the full moon had begun to vanish, a tiny sliver slipping away with the start of the eclipse. Her body against mine, I could feel the pounding of Phoebe's heart. "But tonight's different. I'm different."

"It is," she agreed. "You are." She lifted her head, looked right at me, sapphire eyes meeting my own brown ones. "You chased me for such a long time, my Sun. You should claim your reward, rather than waste time talking."

Her lips were so close. Mine grew dry with anticipation, and I wet them with a flick of the tongue. I was trembling. I had pursued her for months, not knowing why, not understanding what tied us together. "Sun chases Moon," I murmured. "I'm most alive during the day. I work with flowers. I'm named for a sun goddess because my mother thought the name was pretty. And I had to wait for tonight to catch you."

Phoebe was silent, inscrutable, patient, unblinking. I went on. "So many cultures have stories about what happens when Sun and Moon meet. Ways to explain eclipses. Ways to explain the tides, the new moon, the full moon, the harvest moon. What aren't you telling me?"

With one hand still caught in mine, she used the other to trace the line of my jaw. "There is... a Wolf. It will be here soon. If you are strong, we will survive. If you are weak, we will both be devoured. This is how it's always been."

I blinked, processing her words and her touch. It was hard to think when every time our skin met, it sent a new wave of arousal and want straight through me, as if every nocturnal fantasy I'd ever entertained about her had returned to haunt me. "A wolf?"

"A Wolf," she corrected. And this time, I caught how she said it, how the word invoked something primal and unstoppable, eternally hungry and ever on her trail. Something touched on in myths and legends and stories told around campfires of millennia past. "I need you to be strong, Malina. Usually, the Wolf subsists on the memories he strips from my lovers each month, and the life he nibbles from me as I wane. But this is the end of a much longer cycle, one spanning decades and centuries, and there's... more involved. The Wolf will be bolder, and hungrier." She used her free hand to mime the jaws of a beast, snapping the fingers shut sharply. "Perhaps I chose you, or perhaps you were chosen for me, to represent the Sun in all its glory. When I saw you that first time, I knew you were the one." There lay the explanation for so much, with so much more left unspoken.

"What must I do?" I kept my voice from trembling, and was proud of the small victory. There was no doubt that I'd chased myself right into the middle of something vastly older and stranger than my everyday existence; only Phoebe's hand in mine served to comfort and ground me.

Her lips were mere inches away from mine, and I could smell the ancient wild of her breath. I breathed it in, deeply, learning her scent, tingling all over. "Love me tonight. We must feed the Wolf so it does not feed on us."

"Here? Now?" The park wasn't exactly crowded, but the eclipse, now well underway, had drawn a good number of spectators, most of whom were fixated upon the slowly-unfolding spectacle in the sky. Even so, we'd be hard to ignore.

"Here. Now. Under the stars, under the moon. No one will see us. This is not for their eyes, and they will never realize what goes on around them. The Moon is for mysteries." I heard her quiet intensity, and understood that this was no random hook-up, no casual one night stand for her. I wasn't one of the women chosen almost on a whim to maintain her existence. I was here for a purpose. This was important.

I kissed the Moon.

And she kissed me back.

Her energy roared into me, catching every nerve on fire in a way more erotic than painful, and I knew then the risk of catching a goddess. I swept back her silver hair as we kissed, losing a hand in its silken strands, and we melted together, lips parting and tongues dancing. She tasted like moonlight; I drank it in, giving it back to her as sunlight, which she accepted hungrily. Her fingers skimmed over my stomach before resting on my breast, and I moaned, chest arching into the light touch. I'd dreamed of this a hundred times and more, but none of it compared to the reality. I could feel her through my shirt and bra as if they didn't even exist.

I released the hand I'd held captive all this time so I could use both of mine to explore her body, stroking and caressing with wild abandon. She was smooth and sleek, sensually responsive to the slightest touch, her moans crashing against my lips like waves on the shore. She fell back under me, until we lay together on the cool grass, her skirt ridden dangerously high up along pale, bare legs, blouse untucked to expose a generous amount of stomach. Had I done all that without even realizing? It was only when I felt cool air on my arousal-tightened nipples that I realized I was entirely topless, and her hands were everywhere, and when had we stopped kissing to make that happen?

Above us, the moon continued to disappear, now a third gone as the heavens moved with inexorable patience. Below me, the Moon writhed in response to my touch, her breasts bare, so pale they glowed. I captured one erect nipple in my mouth and sucked, drawing forth her mystery while she whimpered. Her nails raked along my back, sending sharp shivers through me. In my dreams, she'd always been the aggressor, I the recipient of her attentions, but now I saw how it had to be. Sun chases Moon. She needed me, needed this. I needed her. I pulled her skirt up to her waist, slipped my hand between her legs and found her bare, soaking, and ready for me. I plunged my fingers into her depths, finding the hot core of her arousal and claiming it at long last. Her muscles tensed, trying to trap me as I stroked and fucked her with my hand, liquid silver moans escaping her parted lips. I met her mouth with mine again, kissing her silent while she thrashed and bucked urgently, accepting all I had to give, and demanding more.

As I poured myself into her with my kiss, and thrust myself into her with my hand, she shone ever brighter, turning night into day while the moon above slipped halfway and more into darkness.

I loved her in that moment, an outpouring of emotion built up over months of unfulfilled pursuit and courtship, loved the vast unknowable mystery that called itself Phoebe Masters, and she drank it all in. Her cries grew insistent against my lips, and I released her mouth just as she came for me. She shuddered, pussy tight around my driving fingers, hips arching, body quivering, then she exploded, silver light streaming out in every direction, coating the grass and bushes and trees and sky with her glow. Overhead, the moon vanished in its entirety, the only hint of time passing while we were occupied.

The world growled, a primal, hungry sound coming from everywhere and nowhere, surrounding us. I felt hot breath on the back of my neck, my hackles rising in the presence of something ancient and feral. I paused, Phoebe still orgasming around my slowing fingers. She grabbed me by the back of my neck before I could pull away to look around, and hissed, "Love me, Malina. Be strong. Don't stop!" This time, her kiss was fierce and demanding, her tongue driving between my lips with renewed purpose, and I gave myself to her. I gave myself to her as the Wolf prowled ever closer, its hungry panting mimicking our own heavy breaths. Its very presence cast a pall on things, a dark shadow that chilled where it touched. I shivered, pressing against Phoebe to share her warmth.

I felt the eyes fixed on the back of my neck. I imagined the teeth, razor-sharp and poised to eat me. I felt them... and I almost froze. Like a rabbit confronted by a predator. I was exposed and vulnerable. The Wolf's shadow fell over me, eclipsing me, and I faltered, breath caught deep in my chest. And it chuckled.

The Wolf was hunger. It was fear. It was intolerance, and bigotry, and hate. It was the shadow in our hearts, and the teeth in our souls. It was superstition and close-mindedness, and the reason I'd left home after graduation. It was vicious rumors and poisoned looks, dead friendships and distant relatives. I saw the Wolf. And I rejected it.

This is me, I told the Wolf, as I kissed Phoebe with all my heart. *I've made new friends, and new family here in Puxhill. I'm happy here. I'm myself. No hiding. No secrets. No lies.* I surrendered myself to Phoebe's questing hands, letting her flip me over and stretch me out. She was every lover I'd ever taken, every moment of happiness I'd known since I embraced my inner self. *Go away, Wolf.* I cast away the Wolf as I had everyone who told me I was wrong, a sinner, unnatural, unclean. I accepted Phoebe as I had the scene at Club Armageddon, the sisterhood of the Rollergirls, the gatherings at Bifrost Books, the Rainbow Alliance at Tuesday University. I'd made my own life, and it did not include letting the Wolf in. *You don't frighten me. You have no power over me.* Wolf would not eat Moon or Sun tonight.

Phoebe took her turn, and her time, with me. She sucked my fingers dry before kissing me, granting me a secondhand taste of her, and I accepted the offering. It was a pale shadow of the real thing, I knew, but even this small sampling was heady and intoxicating. She swiftly rid me of my pants, then bent down to bury her face between my legs, tongue darting out to lap and tease at my clit, electrifying me once more. I clutched at my breasts, pinching the nipples into fullness, taking the pain with the pleasure and finding it all good. The Wolf growled again, and Phoebe's tongue lapped at my pussy, drinking in my Sun-soaked essence while I moaned her name. The Wolf paced around us, and I thrashed and whimpered, the intensity of my passion keeping it at bay. The Wolf howled in frustration, and I screamed with pleasure, drowning it out. As Phoebe sucked at my clit and fucked me with several long, skilled fingers, I threw my head back to worship the Moon, not in words but in a long, inarticulate sound transcending meaning. My orgasm was sudden, violent, and all-consuming. Phoebe reveled in it, the Wolf feasted and the eclipse paused in its tracks for one long moment of eternity.

Then time restarted, and Phoebe held me while my body shook and I tried to catch my breath. Her glow was cool and comforting, her body warm and soft, and she stroked my sides and breasts and hair with gentle hands, whispering to me in a long-dead language. Overhead, a sliver of moon reappeared, and the Wolf's shadow stole away. It wasn't gone yet. The Wolf would never be gone completely; it was hooked too deep into our very nature. Where there's light, there's shadow.

"That was for the Wolf," she whispered, kissing me with surprising tenderness, running her fingers through my hair to untangle it and pick out some stray blades of grass. "This time is for us."

Her touch was gentle, even soothing, cooling the burned places of my soul, a balm to my overstimulated nerves, and yet this was just as erotic as before. That had been born of lust and passion; this was born of love and compassion. She kissed my nipples, she caressed my breasts, she nibbled playfully at my throat, bringing me down from the one high and drawing me to another with an immortal's patience. My fantasies came to life under her slow, playful ministrations, the reward for a job well done. Phoebe guided me to the edge of orgasm, letting me sit there with every muscle tensed and ready, letting me quietly beg for completion, before pushing me over with a single kiss and push of the fingers. I was reborn in her arms, even as the moon emerged from the eclipse once and for all.

The Wolf had vanished, padding away with a full belly. I wondered what impact a meal freely-given would have upon it, if for a time the shadows would be lighter and the nights a little brighter. At any rate, the moment was over. It was just me and Phoebe, Sun and Moon, clinging together in the dying hours of the night, while an unknowing audience packed up and left the park, chattering about what a lovely night it had been for watching an eclipse. Phoebe was renewed, not just for another month, but for decades or centuries to come. I felt a stab deep in my heart when I realized the night was drawing to a close. Still, I had to ask. "What happens now?"

She gave me another soft, knowing smile, and traced my cheek with light fingers. "Sun chases Moon. Moon chases Sun. In between, there's day and night and a world full of life. I think, though, having caught me, you'll find yourself free to choose your own destiny."

"And if I choose to chase you?" I asked.

Her shrug spoke a lifetime of unknowns. "The last time this happened, she didn't want anything to do with me afterward. The Wolf scared her too badly."

"I'm tougher than that," I replied. I'd seen the Wolf and sent it packing once. I could do it again if need be.

"You are, aren't you," she said. "I suppose anything's possible. You might catch me again. Or not. You might suffer a lifetime of yearning in exchange for another night like this, or you might never succeed. I can't say. You might find someone you can be with, and abandon the chase altogether. I can't say."

I sighed, relaxing against her. "You don't like straightforward answers, do you?"

She laughed, and wrapped her arms around me. "I'm afraid it's not my way." And that was that.

Tonight, I kissed the Moon. I don't know what tomorrow brings, but I'm looking forward to it.

The Seduction of the Sea
T.K. Ashley

Lyndsy sank back into the damp patch of clover and remarked upon her surroundings with satisfaction. The ground beneath her was springy with moss and pleasantly warmed by thick rays of sunshine. The white-barked ash trees surrounding her were well-built and of a size substantial enough to obscure the little meadow from view. A gentle breath of wind glided through their leaves, tingeing the air with a hint of salt from the ocean. Just beyond the clearing, the merry bubbling of a brook muffled out all unwelcome sound. It was tranquil, comfortable, and remote. Yes, every facet of this private oasis was ideal to her purposes, and Lyndsy had to congratulate herself on its perfection.

It would be the perfect place to murder a mermaid.

Lyndsy cheerfully plucked off the petals of a flower as she plotted, humming to herself as she pictured the mermaid's glassy eyes widening in terror, her lips opening and closing in horror as Lyndsy made her attack. Lyndsy's revenge would be sweet but slow, and she wouldn't stop until the fish had croaked her last. The idea filled her with a tingling warmth that slithered up and down her spine. She closed her eyes as she indulged in the fantasy, giving a short gasp of longing with every petal she plucked, imagining that each was one of the mermaid's scales. How the bitch would scream with pain! Lyndsy smiled and shifted lazily in the grass, stretching her arms up and clasping her hands behind her head in satisfaction. She was just weighing over what manner of weapon she ought to use to stab the little beast when a voice in the near distance rang out in singsong:

Is that mischief I smell?

— *Farewell! Farewell!*

Is that trouble I hear?

— *Stand clear! Stand clear!*

Is that wicked I taste?

— *Make haste! Make haste!*

The high, clear voice reverberated all around her ears until she found she couldn't determine from which direction it came. She sat up on her elbows and pouted her lips in a pretty frown, tossing her long, blonde hair from side to side as she sought out the source of the voice.

"Who's there?" she called out with irritation.

The echo of a snicker met her ears.

Lyndsy crushed the remains of the hapless flower in her fist. "That better not be who I think it is."

Silence was her only answer.

"Show yourself!" she demanded, gathering the gauzy muslin of her skirts and rising to her knees.

"Make me," a tiny voice taunted.

Lyndsy swung her head over to the sizable elm tree to her left and smiled. He'd betrayed his location. She grabbed for a rock, screwed up one side of her lip in concentration, and then threw the rock with all of her strength at the tree's upper branches. To her satisfaction, the voice issued a violent grunt of pain. Then a small, limp mass barreled through the leaves towards the ground, where it landed in an ungainly heap.

"Ha!" Lyndsy exclaimed in triumph. She leaped up and ran to the crumpled figure's side, where she looked down upon it with not the slightest speck of pity.

At her feet, the injured sprite groaned and rolled over onto his back, bringing a tiny hand up to his mop of wildly red hair and examining his little skull for injury. In everything he was a miniature. The breadth and length of his limbs could stretch no farther than the span of Lyndsy's outstretched hand, and he had sharp, delicate features that might have been carved with the point of pin. All of his parts were harmonious in proportion but his eyes—great, green eyes that turned up at the corner like a cat's—which were entirely too large for such a small face. Currently, those eyes regarded Lyndsy with anger.

"I liked you better when it was only my *feelings* you sought to injure," he pronounced.

Lyndsy tilted her head. "I can't recall *ever* liking you."

The sprite made an indignant noise much too loud for his slight frame, and the force of its shock reverberating through him left him dazed.

Lyndsy snorted, then—intent on her original purpose—swallowed her amusement. "I told you not to spy on me, Eagan. You're lucky I didn't do any worse to you."

"I reckon I *am* lucky since you're already plotting one murder today." Eagan lifted himself unsteadily to his feet and set to brushing off the back of his pants.

Lyndsy concealed her surprise. "I don't know what you're talking about."

Eagan's eyes flashed to hers darkly. "I can smell mischief a league away," he said, then lowered his eyes to the cleft between her legs, where the thin fabric of her skirt had clung and gathered during her movement, "... among other things. And the scent of your, ah, *mischief* is especially pungent."

Lyndsy spluttered, too mortified to speak. Self-conscious, she shook out her skirt so that it no longer clung to her legs, but—to her humiliation—the slight friction only furthered her discomfort. She clamped her thighs together, hoping that would settle the matter.

"So, who are you planning to kill?" Eagan asked casually, as if he were inquiring as to whom she planned to invite to her next dinner party.

Lyndsy's embarrassment was soon forgotten. "That little fish bitch," she said through clenched teeth.

"Who, Narissa?" Eagan asked, looking up at her curiously. "Why?"

There were so many reasons. Everything about her was odious. From the way her voice rang like wind chimes, to the impossible length of her eyelashes, to the infuriating buoyancy of her round, perky...

"Now *that* smells like jealousy," Eagan observed.

Lyndsy balked. "I'm not jealous of her!"

"Oh, hmm, perhaps I was wrong." Eagan wrinkled his nose, then grinned up at her wickedly. "Maybe it's lust I'm smelling."

Lyndsy reached down to throttle the sprite, but he deftly leaped aside, laughing merrily. "It's true! It's true!" he whooped with delight and clapped his little hands together.

Lyndsy sank to her knees, her arms crossed in a chokingly tight vise across her breasts, the peaks of which were traitorously hardened by his suggestion. "It is not true," she bit out. "Though I'm probably the only person in the whole damned village not taken in by her." Lyndsy, a pretty girl in her own right, was not used to being ignored, but ever since the mermaid Narissa had taken up roost in the neighboring cove, Lyndsy couldn't even attract an extended handshake from a man, much less anything more satisfying.

"Mmhmm. So, not-jealousy and not-lust are the reasons you've taken off work to plot her demise alone in this meadow. You're right—this is probably the best excuse for a sick day that I can think of," Eagan said.

"What's the point in opening the shop? What need has anyone for potions when there's a mermaid's spell to fall under? Besides, Master Tallis hasn't been in house in weeks, and the most I can muster without his supervision is wart salve." Like the rest of the men (and even some women) in the village, Master Tallis spent his days down at the cove, mooning and fawning over Narissa as she played a song on her harp or combed her long, raven hair. All semblances of production and commerce were shut down, and the village was propelled back into the Dark Ages, its people content to subsist on wild berries and the sweet sound of Narissa's voice.

It made Lyndsy sick.

"Hey, people need wart salve," Eagan argued.

"Maybe, but they don't need *me*." Lyndsy looked around for another flower to dismember, found none, and settled for ripping up random fistfuls of grass.

Eagan frowned. "To be fair, I doubt they need Narissa very much either."

By the resulting hiss Lyndsy uttered, Eagan surmised that he had answered wrongly.

"I mean to say," he amended quickly, "that they need you a lot more than they need Narissa. You're useful. You help people. She's just a pretty bauble to look at."

"People don't want to be helped. People want to be flattered, which Narissa does every time she swings that ridiculous mane of hair over one fishy shoulder and titters that gurgly laugh at someone's bad joke. People *want* Narissa—they don't want me."

Eagan considered questioning her as to how exactly Narissa's grisly murder would sway more people to Lyndsy's favor, but decided on a different route of discourse. "That's not true. I want you," he said.

Lyndsy dropped the fistful of mutilated grass. "You do?" she asked, almost suspiciously. Her sky blue eyes narrowed to slits as she watched him for signs of deceit.

He shrugged his shoulders as if this information ought to be obvious. "Of course I do! You're smart, beautiful, oh-so-fun to be around... and besides—your mischief smells the sweetest."

Eagan's quick reflexes allowed him to avoid a backhand from Lyndsy, however the resulting wind from her swift movement knocked him clear onto his back. "Will you *stop* trying to injure me?" he protested from the ground. "Mercy, is it any wonder you chase people away with an attitude like that? I was paying you a compliment!"

"Keep your compliments to yourself," Lyndsy grumbled as she cracked her knuckles, which were sore from being held in fists too long.

Eagan sat up on his elbows. "Easy, Lyndsy. Don't you ever relax?"

Lyndsy thought bitterly of how much more she'd be relaxing had he not intruded on her privacy. "Yes. I do relax. When I'm *alone*."

"Oh come on, sweets. You're too tense. Let me rub your shoulders."

"No."

"Your feet?"

"Not even if you had normal sized hands."

"Your... mischief?" His green eyes twinkled naughtily.

Lyndsy flushed. "Don't be disgusting, Eagan! You're..." she gestured inadequately with her hand, "incredibly tiny!"

"I bet I could fit your relevant bit in my mouth." He waggled his eyebrows suggestively.

Lyndsy made an exasperated noise. "I'm not *that* desperate. Thanks for asking."

Actually, she *was* that desperate. Lyndsy hadn't so much as touched another person in almost a month—if you don't count the swollen glands of Master Tallis' patients. And even *that* intimate contact produced nothing more than a polite tip of the patient's hat.

"What—you don't think I could please you?"

"You're joking, right?" Lyndsy wasn't sure if he was teasing her or just being thick. "I've had dildos bigger than you! What are you planning to do? Go spelunking in my crevice while you juggle your own bits? Nice try, Eagan. I'd rather fuck the fish."

"Oh, I bet you would." Eagan laughed uproariously, the high-pitched sound tinny and mocking to Lyndsy's ears.

"Ha. Ha. Just—just leave me alone." Lyndsy turned around, her face bright red with anger, embarrassment, and frustration.

Eagan stopped laughing. "I'm serious, you know. I can pleasure you," he said, his tone ripe with promises.

Lyndsy was almost revolted at herself at the thrill that passed through her body at his words. "Don't you have a fairy to fondle or something?" she joked, but her voice was muffled in her ears, overpowered by the sudden hammering of her heart.

"Close your eyes."

Lyndsy shivered unbidden at his words, which seemed to be spoken right behind her ear. She didn't know why, but she obeyed him, fluttering her eyelids closed uncertainly and shifting awkwardly in place. "Alright," she said gamely. "But if I turn around and you're naked, I'll decapitate you with my teeth."

He laughed, but the sound was so much deeper and louder

than usual that she half wondered if someone else had come into the clearing. She opened her eyes. "Eagan?" she called uncertainly as she sensed a presence looming behind her.

"Yes?" a pleasant tenor asked, its warm mouth exploring the outer shell of her ear.

Lyndsy screamed and whirled around, only to be caught in the arms of a man who looked *strangely* like Eagan—only in proper, normal-man proportions.

"Relax," human Eagan laughed, his smile broadening to a grin. "It's me, sweets."

She stared at him in shock, her jaw gaping as she struggled to comprehend. It was Eagan, and yet... he was someone else entirely. She never would have seen how truly handsome he was at his former size. His unruly, red hair fell at uneven lengths down to the angle of his pointed jaw. His features were delicate—almost feminine—but the cut of his mouth was rougher, fuller. Even though he was kneeling, she could see his lean body easily out-measured her in height. His shirt had been spun of spider silk and fell open casually at the neck, revealing a smooth chest that while not broad, was hardened with strength. His pants, woven from dried flax, molded naturally to the long line of his legs, and were fastened around his narrow hips by what must have been twine in its original dimensions but now looked like the thick riggings of a ship. She found herself staring at the conspicuous swell of fabric beneath the line of his belt, and couldn't help wondering whether the same transformation in size that had been applied to the rest of his body had manifested there as well.

His green eyes, still curiously large for his face, turned a deep emerald as he watched her take in his appearance, and his gaze seemed to penetrate straight through the flimsy fabric of her dress. "Everything is in proportion," he said, answering her unspoken question. "Some proportions being more generous than others." He lowered his voice conspiratorially as he said, "I'm talking about my cock, of course."

Lyndsy was too curious to be angry with him for trying to

discomfit her. "But how did you...?" she started to ask, puzzling out how this alteration had come about. She had, of course, seen Eagan perform any number of magical pranks before, but she had never even known he was capable of such large-scale magic, much less been witness to it.

"I have a lot of tricks up my sleeve," he said. He twirled her in his arms and pulled her back against his chest, parting his legs to settle her between his thighs. "You just never care to see them."

His embrace was so warm and inviting that Lyndsy couldn't help but sink back into his arms, which surrounded her with the tangy aromas of grass and leaves and bark—all manners of scents that made her feel as if she were leaning back against the trunk of a tree instead of a man.

"Oh," she said lamely, giving herself over a little to his seduction. Her eyes drifted closed as Eagan's new, human-sized hands moved to her shoulders and began to massage away the hardened knots beneath her skin. "But I've never seen you..." she began to protest.

"Shhhh," he said, his breath passing lightly over her ear. "Don't worry about me. Why don't you tell me why Narissa's got a bee in your bonnet? Did she steal your beau?"

But Lyndsy couldn't *help* but worry about Eagan as his capable fingers slid down from her shoulders to caress along the underside of her collarbones. "I don't have a beau," she said, willing her voice to be calmer than she felt. Eagan had tucked his face into the hollow of her shoulder as he worked his fingers in slow, wide arcs that drifted ever downward over the plane of her breastbone, and his breath came warm and teasing against the side of her neck. Lyndsy's voice caught slightly as she kept talking, "It's not just because she's... beautiful." Her eyes flew open as one of Eagan's fingers skimmed the top of her bodice, but she continued, "I can't stand the way she's manipulating the whole village. They'd starve to death before they'd leave her side. It's a mercy she goes to bed at sea to rest at night, otherwise they'd all have wasted away to nothing."

"And you're the only one who realizes this?" Eagan mumbled

against her neck, his lips brushing against her skin not quite in a kiss, but not quite by accident either.

"I must be," Lyndsy admitted, her eyelids drooping. Eagan was spinning some kind of magic around her—she could feel it enveloping and exploring her—but she didn't care. It felt so good. "At least, if anyone else notices, they aren't doing anything about it."

"So what are you going to do about it?" Eagan was fingering the bow at the neckline of Lyndsy's gown. He pulled the threading apart delicately, allowing the garment to bloom open over her breasts, which sat high and tense with anticipation.

"Stop her," Lyndsy gasped as Eagan peeled the open neckline of her gown down her shoulders, fully exposing her breasts. "Before she hurts anyone else."

"How?" Eagan prodded, taking her earlobe delicately between his teeth.

Lyndsy was keenly aware of Eagan's hand as it made its torturous way down the center of her breastbone. "Well, first: I'll drag her to this clearing, where I'll pin her down by her hands and flippers. Then: I'll get out my assortment of rocks and pointed sticks."

"Mmhmm," Eagan mumbled absently. He palmed one of her breasts, weighing it in his hand thoughtfully as he listened to her plan of attack. "Suppose she resists? I hear mermaid teeth are quite sharp." He pinched Lyndsy's nipple, earning a surprised cry of pain from her. "Suppose she bites you," he said, opening his jaw over the tender line of her throat.

Lyndsy suppressed a gurgle of approval. "She won't. I'll gag her with her own hair if I have to."

"Then you won't be able to hear her scream." Eagan covered her other breast, kneading and squeezing the pair of them together and apart, then roughly pulling and pinching her nipples between his fingers. "Or beg for mercy."

Lyndsy felt her mouth fall slack as Eagan groped her openly. She let her hands drop down to his knees on either side of her, her own legs parting as she relaxed. The air around her clouded with the magic Eagan was weaving, and she breathed it in deeply, gratefully. She could feel desire creeping through her veins like a drug, spreading from the crown of her head down the lengths of her arms, over the tips of her breasts in Eagan's capable hands and across the plane of her stomach, where it suddenly bottomed out and rushed headlong to her eager sex. "Eagan," she gasped out, begging for mercy herself as her arousal pooled warm and slick between her legs.

"Shh," Eagan said. "We were talking about Narissa—not me," he said, as if she could ignore his hands moving down to her waist. He gripped her hips and pulled her back hard against the unmistakable bulge of his stiffened cock. "What do you want to do to her once she's tied up and at your fearsome mercy?"

Lyndsy reflected on this scenario with pleasure. She imagined Narissa's hands tied above her head, displaying her perfect breasts to their best advantage as they heaved with her gasps of fear. The very idea set the inner walls of her pussy to a pulse. Lyndsy was taken aback momentarily by her own reaction. She wanted to punish the mermaid, not pleasure her! Then Lyndsy relaxed when she realized this was probably just part of Eagan's naughty spell. Bastard. All the same something had to be done about this maddening need. She tried to push back against Eagan's cock to encourage him to touch her some more, but he kept his hands and her hips firmly in place, waiting for her to answer. "Then I'll stab her straight through her scaly heart," Lyndsy said, placing her hands over Eagan's and trying to push them down lower to where she needed them most.

"Through her heart? But what a waste of such great little tits." As he spoke he shook off Lyndsy's hands and lifted his own to caress her breasts again. "No, you'll have to stab her elsewhere."

Appeased slightly by his course of action, she tried again for the right answer. "Through her slimy gut then." But she wasn't thinking of stabbing the mermaid as she pictured Narissa's taut abdomen in her mind. Instead, inexplicably, she imagined placing her own hands around the narrow circle of her waist and drawing her closer.

As if he were privy to her thoughts, Eagan's hands mimicked Lyndsy's in her peculiar fantasy, leaving her breasts and smoothing down over what remained of her bodice over her stomach. "Very intimate," he remarked, beginning to gather the fabric of her dress between his fingers, inching it higher and higher up her calves. "But also on the messy side. Have you ever gutted a fish? Not the easiest thing to clean up. You'll have scales under your nails for weeks."

Lyndsy was beginning to detect a correlation between her own suggestions and Eagan's hands, and so she schemed desperately for a way to guide his fingers to a more satisfying location. "Then I guess I'll just have to stab her up her fishy slit," she blurted out, her cheeks immediately coloring as she realized how ridiculous that sounded. She wasn't even sure mermaids *had* slits.

"You're beginning to sound rather ghoulish, sweets. When a woman says she wants to stab another woman in the muff, it's enough to put one off his breakfast." Eagan reached with his fingertips to the newly exposed flesh of Lyndsy's knees and began to trail them upwards. "What do you suppose mermaid bits even taste like?" Eagan asked, seizing upon a more palatable subject. "I imagine it's rather like gargling sardines. If I were you, I'd just ask her to go down on *you* instead."

Lyndsy cried out both in protest and pleasure as Eagan's fingers whispered over the swollen folds of her sex and then retreated back down her leg. "I didn't say anything about tasting anyone's bits," she said, twisting awkwardly in his arms to glare at him.

"Maybe not," he said slyly, "but you're thinking about it now." The corners of his unnaturally large eyes crinkled with laughter. "And I bet your mischief tastes sweet." He brought one of his hands to the back of her head and guided her face to his in a kiss.

Despite her annoyance with him, Lyndsy couldn't resist the tender brush of his mouth against hers, so she gave in, turning herself further in his embrace to wrap an arm around his neck. The sprite's lips were as rough and demanding as they were pliant, his kiss spiced with wild mint and sun-warmed clover. As he moved his tongue to part her lips, his nimble fingers spread the folds of her sex, seeking the hardened bud of her clitoris. Lyndsy moaned into his mouth as he stroked her—just once—and Eagan's spell was complete. She would gladly consent to bedding a whole pod of mermaids if it meant she could just have more of this feeling right this minute.

She broke the kiss and pushed him back onto the mossy ground, scrambling to move on top of him despite the cumbersome burden of her skirts. "Don't say a fucking thing," she snapped in response to the immensely self-satisfied expression on Eagan's face as he watched her fumble open the rope belt at his waist. She felt her hand inside his pants for the rigid length of his cock and something inside her long-neglected sex twitched in response.

"Give me something to do with my mouth and I won't say a word," he promised, sliding his tongue over his lips in a lewd suggestion. He moved his hand to cover her fingers around his cock and added, "I can take care of this end."

At this point Lyndsy would have been willing to hump a walrus to soothe the aching need between her legs, so finding an excuse to wipe that cocksure grin off of Eagan's face was only an added bonus in favor of this course of action. She returned his wicked smile and crawled over his torso on her hands and knees, stopping above his shoulders and bunching up her skirts into two wads by her waist. She planted her knees on either side of his head and waited, with heart-pounding anticipation, for him to make the next move.

He turned his face to one side and nuzzled the inside of her thigh, breathing in deeply. "Oh, sweet mischief!" were the last words he uttered before setting his mouth to the task of pleasing her.

"Oh!" Lyndsy cried as his tongue swept up the length of her slit and curled a teasing loop around her clitoris. She found she much preferred this application of his wagging tongue to his earlier teasing, even more so because she couldn't see his mocking face under the bunch of her skirts. And so she was free to imagine whatever she liked between her thighs, whichever tongue she pleased flicking back and forth over her bud, being worried to a frenzy between whomever's lips she desired.

To her shock, the only such person she could think of in this context was the mermaid Narissa.

"You bitch," Lyndsy hissed to herself—to Eagan—to Narissa. Eagan must be making her think this way, for surely such an idea could never have come from her own mind. Yet even the thought of Narissa's salty tongue lapping at her pussy didn't stop Lyndsy from gently lifting and dropping her hips over Eagan's mouth, grinding herself against his skilled tongue. Now she imagined it was Narissa's hand groping her backside, sliding her fingers towards the entrance of Lyndsy's throbbing sex. "You *bitch*," Lyndsy repeated in a growl, even as she leaned forward to grant better access to what she knew were Eagan's fingers.

Eagan made a throaty sound halfway between a laugh and a moan as he worked his cock to a lather in the grip of his free hand. He urged her faster with his tongue as he pumped two fingers mercilessly in and out of her, and he smiled privately to himself as she abandoned all pretense and began to cry out in earnest. Her thighs were tense and trembling on either side of his face as he curled his fingers inside her pussy, bringing her screaming to a shuddering halt above him.

Lyndsy collapsed forward onto her hands, her breath coming in the hard, heart-pounding gasps of the recently satisfied. She spread her legs wider as she felt Eagan squirming underneath her, lifted her chest to allow him to wriggle up so that their faces were even. "That was..." She hesitated, wondering how much gratitude she was compelled to bestow upon someone she normally found so bothersome.

"Not over yet," he finished for her, arching his hips high and hard as he guided his cock between her overheated folds and into her passage.

Lyndsy gasped as his thick member filled her, and she dropped and angled her hips to better accommodate him. The aftershocks of her climax caused her walls to contract pleasurably around his cock as he worked it deeper into her. "Narissa," she moaned, and he didn't correct her. Narissa's bewitching face and breasts and tongue were soon forgotten as Eagan clutched her hips and thrust harder and faster up into her. Lyndsy lowered her face to watch him, her blonde hair tumbling around them and trapping them in a private embrace. Whether it was his spell or his cock working its magic over her, Lyndsy couldn't stop staring at Eagan's handsome face as it twisted with unvoiced pleasure. She found herself throwing her hips back against his, trying to unnerve him as much as he had her. Her blue eyes lit up with triumph as he groaned beneath her, and she clenched her sex firmly around his cock as it stiffened and he spilled into her.

No sooner had Lyndsy leaned in to trail a post-coital kiss behind Eagan's ear than she found herself flat on her face with a mouthful of moss. She spat violently and lifted herself on her elbows, looking around with bewilderment. "What the hell?" she wondered aloud.

"Over here," a small voice said, and she whipped her head down to the ground near her left elbow, where the little sprite sat gulping in as much air as his tiny lungs could hold. "Sorry, that tends to... happen... if I try to hold human form too long," he said, his tone deflated.

The spell was broken. Lust left her and irritation returned. "Why did you make me think those things about Narissa?" she demanded angrily, reaching to put her dress to rights as quickly as her shaking fingers would allow her. The fog of Eagan's magic had cleared from her mind, replaced instead by a grating headache.

He grinned up at her, making no move to cover what parts of him were still exposed. "I thought you'd thank me for that," he said with a shrug of his shoulders.

Flustered, Lyndsy clung to her rage to spare her dignity. "Why would you think I wanted anything of the kind? I want to kill that creature, not romance it!" She stood up and immediately her annoyance was renewed by the sensation of Eagan's sticky release oozing down the inside of her thigh. How could she have willingly lain with someone so insufferable? She wasn't sure the skill of his amorous attentions outweighed the humiliation of his taunting.

"I'm not entirely sure you know *what* it is you want," Eagan said, finally reaching down to tie his belt closed. "All I know is that while I can suggest quite a lot, I can't *make* you do anything. So!" he said, hopping lightly to his feet and clapping his hands together authoritatively. "Let's get a move on, shall we? We've got a sea cow to slay and only a few more hours of daylight to do it! Come on—I know a shop that sells silver-tipped daggers at a reasonable sum..." Eagan bent his knees and gave a mighty leap, sending him soaring with unnatural agility to the lowest branch of the elm tree.

"Alright," Lyndsy grumbled as she followed after him. As he flitted from branch to branch in the trees ahead of her, she tried to sort out the tangle of emotions running through her. What Eagan had said was true: she wasn't sure what she wanted anymore. Narissa was evil—of that she was certain—but why did she feel such an unholy attraction to the mermaid? Lyndsy couldn't decide whether she wanted more to kill her or kiss her, and indecision soured like indigestion in her gut. One thing was clear: only one of them would leave the encounter alive.

The shore was a dark, wriggling mass at sunset. The people of Lyndsy's village were crammed together over every available space the narrow, rocky beach could afford. They were, of the main, unwashed, their clothing disheveled, and their bodies and faces blended together in one indiscriminate mass of slackened jaws and watching eyes. Half a league away their boats bobbed untended in the harbor, their fishing nets left dried and unused in the fading sun. The villagers sat still—some swaying slightly, some humming along—their entire being focused on the mermaid Narissa.

She was perched on a low rock formation in the center of the cove. Her long, piscine tail curled around the rock's base and dipped in the water, its length glittering with dull, pewter scales that reflected the sheen of the darkening ocean. Her heavy drape of black hair was twisted into a loose braid over one shoulder, and was dotted with jewels and flower petals she had plucked from her admirers' offerings. Her spindly fingers picked a tune from the harp butted between her small breasts as she sang a haunting melody in words that no one understood. Behind her, the sun slowly sank towards its watery bed for the night.

Lyndsy hesitated at the edge of the woods, half-concealed by the trunk of a large oak, and watched the scene before her with despair.

"I'll wait for you here," Eagan informed her, settling into a high knot on the tree's trunk.

Lyndsy snapped her eyes away from the mermaid and up to the sprite. "What?" she asked, her pitch heightened to a squeak. "You're just going to let me go alone?" All the determination she'd mustered in the clearing was starting to waver; in her trembling hands a velvet purse shook slightly.

"Fancy lot of good I'd do you if I did go. My magic doesn't work outside of the forest, and with my luck Lady Mackerel will mistake me for a minnow and have me for a midnight snack," he said with a shudder, then reconsidered, "Although... there *are* worse things than going down such a beautiful throat—am I right?" Even in the face of this serious situation, Eagan started snickering.

Lyndsy was very sorry that the sprite was not within striking distance. "Is it at all possible for you to be serious? Even for just a small second? Such as when your friend is about to meet her doom?" She ventured a nervous glance back to the mermaid, who had finished her song and was bowing graciously to the overwhelming applause of her captive audience.

Eagan brightened. "Oh, so now I'm a *friend?*" The idea seemed to please him. "Very well. I shall be sorry to see you die, Lyndsy. Perhaps you'd favor me with a good-bye kiss?" He squeezed his oversized eyes shut and pronounced his lips in a melodramatic pucker.

Lyndsy ignored him, pleaded with what gods may be to protect her, and took a step out of the forest.

"Good luck," Eagan's tiny voice called after her, and—to Lyndsy's surprise—he sounded sincere.

She gripped the velvet pouch a little tighter as she walked towards the gathered crowd. No one even turned to look at her as she gently nudged them aside; their eyes were as focused as Lyndsy's were on Narissa.

But Narissa was not so blind. She set down her harp and swung her braid over to her other shoulder, her olive green eyes narrowing with interest over Lyndsy.

Who are you?

Lyndsy was physically startled as the mermaid's high, melodious voice echoed strangely between her ears. Narissa's lips never moved.

Every face in the crowd turned suddenly to Lyndsy. Among them she saw the familiar features of her old friends and neighbors—she could see Master Tallis was there as well—but something in their looks was alien. Lyndsy felt a chill pass through her that was unwarranted by the mild sea breeze. Their cheeks had become lean and hard with fatigue and hunger. Their hollow eyes reflected nothing of their former selves.

Who are you? the mermaid insisted. She sat up a little higher on her rock perch and coiled her tail closer to her body, the wide fan of its fin twitching with annoyance. Even in her displeasure she was lovely to behold. She could have been sculpted from the stone itself for as proudly as she held herself, yet for as hard as her features were they were offset by the softness of her mouth and the depth of her gaze, which held one captive with all the gravity of a gorgon. She was perfection and poison molded neatly in one.

Lyndsy could not rip her eyes away from the beautiful creature, and so it was blindly that she reached into the velvet pouch she carried.

"She has a weapon!" someone yelled with alarm. "Stop her!"

All at once the crowd surged inward on Lyndsy and she raised her hands over her head in defense. "Wait!" she cried. "It is a gift!"

Indeed, clutched in one of Lyndsy's unsteady hands was an object.

"Come here," the mermaid said aloud, her speaking voice was heavily accented, as if rusty from disuse.

The crowd made no move to part for her, so Lyndsy had to elbow her way through the throngs of people to get to the water's edge, where an unseen pair of hands shoved her hard towards the rising surf. She slipped, and the crowd behind her laughed cruelly as she plunged headfirst into the shallow water. Lyndsy rose to her feet with what decorum she could muster, and the brackish water that dripped down her body heated to a boil with the rising temperature of her anger.

The object in her hand remained intact, and she gripped it tighter with resolve.

What gift do you bring me? the mermaid Narissa asked with no little curiosity. Her eyes scanned Lyndsy's body with undiscriminating severity, pausing over the bodice of her dress, which now clung wet and translucent to her breasts.

Lyndsy's disloyal body responded with enthusiasm to Narissa's inspection, her nipples hardening to dark points beneath the thin, wet fabric of her dress as she waded slowly through the water. Her skirts floated up and formed an unceremonious train behind her as she marched forward, as a bride to the devil's altar. But Lyndsy was no longer afraid as she approached the mermaid's rock. Instead, a cool thrill of anticipation rose higher and higher within her, as did the level of cold seawater, which at first came up to her knees, then to her thighs, and then lapped teasingly against the mouth of her sex. Her earlier romp with Eagan had done nothing but whet her appetite, but this—*she*—was the main course she'd been craving.

The tide washed a taunting wave over her belly as she came to a stop before the mermaid's rock, and Lyndsy waited for Narissa to make the next move.

Narissa smiled at her knowingly as she slithered down from

her perch and glided into the water. *You don't answer me*, she said privately in Lyndsy's mind. *You are afraid of me.* The mermaid came to a stop in front of Lyndsy, treading water as easily as if she were standing, the fan of her tail brushing Lyndsy's bare ankles as it moved. Narissa reached out with her long, delicate fingers and pushed back a lock of Lyndsy's hair, causing a slight tremor to pass through the pair of them. *You are different than the other humans*, Narissa observed, obviously as surprised by her own reaction to Lyndsy as the other woman was by hers.

Lyndsy nearly dropped the object in her hand as Narissa continued to explore the contours of her face with her fingertips. Gone were her plans to confront the mermaid in front of the crowd, to demand she account for the wrongs she had committed against the village, and to threaten her with violence should she choose to continue in her torment. Lyndsy's mouth struggled to speak the words she'd intended, but the only words she could choke out were: "You are very beautiful."

This delighted the mermaid, who rewarded her by dipping one of her graceful fingers between Lyndsy's parted lips. To Lyndsy's dismay, she found herself licking and sucking the mermaid's fingertip, relishing the salty taste of her skin. Narissa closed her eyes briefly and hummed with approval, then repeated her question: *What gift have you brought me?* The mermaid spread her other hand over Lyndsy's closed fist by her side.

Before Lyndsy could protest, Narissa had pried open her fingers and taken the object from her.

Both women looked down at Narissa's open palm, where an intricately carved comb of ivory lay, its handle crusted with tiny flowers wrought of rose gold and pearls. Its tines flashed unmistakably like silver in the setting sun. The mermaid looked up at Lyndsy, her olive eyes darkening with realization. *You meant to hurt me*, she said, but her tone was flavored more with disappointment than anger.

Lyndsy didn't reply, suddenly ashamed of her previous bloodlust. Her heart thudded with dread at what method of punishment the mermaid might choose to inflict upon her. She thought back to the craven little sprite Eagan waiting for her in the big oak tree, and half-regretted not accepting his offer of a good-bye kiss.

To her astonishment, Narissa made no move to censure her. Instead, the mermaid turned her head to one side and smoothed back a few strands of loose hair. *Will you put it on?* she asked, holding out the ivory comb to Lyndsy.

The small request was as unexpected as it was impossible to deny. Lyndsy stepped closer to the mermaid, her breasts tightening with the knowledge that they were but inches from Narissa's pert tits, which glistened enticingly with the spray of the crashing surf. Lyndsy raised her hand, which remained admirably steady, to take the small comb from Narissa's palm and slide it into place above the mermaid's ear. As she was bringing her hand back down, she couldn't help but slide it over the silky braid of the mermaid's hair, her hand pausing at the braid's tip over Narissa's waist.

The crowd, who—unable to hear any of their silent conversation—had been watching with increasing anxiety, cried out in protest as Lyndsy's hand touched the mermaid's satiny skin. "You can't touch her!" someone shouted, and a few made signs of moving forward to stop her.

Narissa turned to them sharply and hissed, her eyes ferocious and commanding. The crowd demurred, but Lyndsy could still feel the heat of their glares on the back of her head.

The mermaid turned back to Lyndsy with the trace of a smile on her lips. *You are curious,* she said, swimming closer to Lyndsy in encouragement. *As am I.*

With Narissa's implied permission, Lyndsy lifted her hands in awe to cup the mermaid's small breasts, marveling as she brushed her thumbs over the erect nipples at how she could have ever fantasized about marring them with a dagger. The mermaid arched into her touch, and Lyndsy rolled her nipples between her fingers in response. She was amazed at Narissa's reaction to her. Could such an enchanting creature as Narissa really desire her?

When the mermaid made no indication of objecting, Lyndsy lowered her hands next to Narissa's flat belly, taking pleasure in the way her slick skin yielded to her gentle touch. As she traced the indentation of Narissa's navel with one thumb, she was horrified that she had ever dreamed of splitting this magnificent skin in anger. She recounted her next suggested point of attack— Narissa's sex—and blushed immediately. And yet.... Her curious hand drifted lower once more, beneath the line of water and over the smooth scales below Narissa's waist. She hesitated with her hand resting over the place a human pubis would lay.

I am as much a woman as you are, Narissa responded mutely to her unvoiced question, guiding Lyndsy's fingers with her own down to the small slit where the mermaid's scales parted. She may have looked like a fish, but Lyndsy found only the heated flesh of a woman beyond the opening; with awe she dipped her fingers into a *woman's* tight passage, and swept her thumb over a *woman's* clitoral bud. Narissa gave a gasp of pleasure and bucked into the other woman's hand as she stroked her slowly, experimentally, under the cover of the water. *Only, without legs,* Narissa continued, her own hand moving between Lyndsy's thighs underwater. She touched the fabric over Lyndsy's pussy with wonder. *Do you really have hair there?*

Lyndsy could answer only in a quiet moan. She wrapped her free arm around Narissa's waist to support herself as the mermaid's hand found its way beneath Lyndsy's skirts to explore her further. The pair of them must have appeared to be locked in a bizarre embrace to the onlookers back on the shore, who were not privy to the succession of stroking and petting and pinching occurring beneath the rising waves. It was like making love to the ocean herself as each undulation of Narissa's body against Lyndsy's rocked her back and forth like the tide, rendering her as relaxed and weightless as a buoy adrift at sea.

She felt Narissa's body begin to tremble in her arms, and then the mermaid cried out. She threw both of her arms around Lyndsy's neck as her orgasm overcame her, her pussy clenching around Lyndsy's fingers, her powerful tail wrapped around one of Lyndsy's legs. Lyndsy brought both hands up to either side of the mermaid's face and leaned down to kiss her, the salty taste of her mouth doing nothing to quench the burning want in the pit of her own belly. Narissa returned the kiss with passion, her cool tongue soft and probing as it moved against Lyndsy's. The grip of her arms relaxed and her hands moved down to caress Lyndsy's body.

Lyndsy sighed and drew her hands down the mermaid's cheeks to her neck. Suddenly, she gasped and pulled away from the mermaid's kiss. Narissa looked back at her wildly, confused, her lips still parted and flushed with pleasure.

Beneath the line of the mermaid's jaw Lyndsy felt two, slender gills.

Comprehension crashed over Lyndsy like a tidal wave. All the while Eagan had taunted her in the meadow about Narissa's anatomy, *he had known*. He had known that the mermaid would use seduction as her weapon of choice. And he had known that stabbing her in the chest, the gut, or anywhere else would be ineffectual.

The mermaid's weakness lay in her gills.

Anger and revulsion swept through her at the mermaid's cunning. In seconds Lyndsy had ripped the silver-tipped comb from the mermaid's hair and pinned the creature back against the rock. Narissa, still sluggish from her climax, did not have time to react, and only emitted a startled whimper as Lyndsy pressed the comb threateningly against her throat. "You tricked me," Lyndsy spat out with venom. "But I know your weakness now."

Behind them the crowd murmured with unease, but, unable to tell whether intervening would earn them a rebuke from Narissa or not, they elected to stay in place.

Narissa choked and coughed as Lyndsy covered one gill with the handle of the comb. *Don't do this*, the mermaid protested. *I did not trick you.* The fire that had been in her eyes earlier had died down, and real fear replaced it. *Please.*

The big, bad, wicked mermaid was begging her for mercy. Something inside of Lyndsy broke at the mermaid's pleading, and a dull ache rose up in her throat. She couldn't do this. Maybe it was selfish, but she couldn't bring herself to take something so beautiful from the world. "You've wronged this village," Lyndsy said, her voice tremulous with feeling. She brought her other hand up to cup the mermaid's face.

I know, the mermaid said, leaning into Lyndsy's touch. I'm sorry.

Lyndsy had trouble believing the mermaid was truly sorry. "You have to leave," she insisted, even as her own heart sank.

I know, Narissa agreed. Impulsively, she leaned forward to give Lyndsy's lips one more kiss, and Lyndsy dropped the comb, knowing she'd never use it to harm the mermaid.

Narissa pulled away from Lyndsy and turned to the shocked onlookers, who knew not what to think. "I must leave you," Narissa announced in her stilted voice.

The crowd protested violently, but she held up one slim hand to quiet them. "Good-bye."

Together with the crowd, Lyndsy watched helplessly as Narissa gathered her harp and began to swim to the cove's entrance. Just before she disappeared beneath the ocean's waves, she looked back at Lyndsy, her sad eyes flaring up with sudden ardor. I'll be back, she promised, one side of her mouth quirking up with amusement. But only for you.

Lyndsy's sex still ached with unattained release, and the promise in Narissa's eyes sizzled straight through her. She did her best to return the mermaid's smile through her discomfort, but as soon as Narissa ducked her ebony head beneath the water Lyndsy hurried back to shore, navigating her way past the dazed villagers, who had woken from the spell in confusion. She hurried past them before they could question her, on a mission to find Eagan.

The little sprite was clucking with disapproval when she found him. "Well, isn't that wonderful. You know this is going to do nothing to quell those rumors that you'll sleep with *anything*."

She considered pointing out that his insult didn't reflect well on him either, then thought better of it and smiled sweetly. "Eagan, follow me. I'm in the mood for... mischief."

The sprite jumped up as if his pants had been lit on fire. "Why didn't you say so in the first place?" he exclaimed, jumping off the branch and into Lyndsy's waiting palm.

She rolled her eyes. Much as she hated to admit it, if she expected to survive until Narissa's return with her sanity intact, she was going to need a helping hand—however tiny.

"But I'm really going to have to insist you wash your hand off first, sweets." Eagan wrinkled up his little nose in disgust. "It smells of live bait."

Lyndsy tucked the ivory comb down the front of her bodice with her free hand. "You'd better get used to it," she said with a private smile, daydreaming about a brilliant pair of olive green eyes.

Become the Mystery
Kara Owl

The sunlight flickering through the palm trees nearby cast shadows that framed the UPS guy's ass nicely, and Audra knew better than to listen when Janice got going, so she tuned her friend out and admired the man's strut as he crossed the street, heading away from their small café. She had just begun drifting into a nice fantasy of meeting him at the door wearing very little when Janice snapped her fingers in Audra's face.

"Hello? I mean, I don't blame you, a man with that much muscle is a thing to be admired, but did you hear a word I said?"

"Sorry, Jan. I don't know what got into me." Jan laughed, and Audra knew she'd managed to dodge a lecture this time. She took a victory sip of her tea and sat back in the comfortable chairs, one of the benefits of this particular spot, wondering what scheme she was going to get caught up into this time. Jan had demanded a meeting this morning, saying that there was something that Audra 'would die for,' and after two days of wibbling, she'd finally agreed to come out. The wibbling had been because Jan's last scheme had been trying to fix Audra up with a string of dates, each one a worse match than the one before. Audra still hadn't figured out a good way to tell Jan that she wasn't ready to date again.

"Well, I have the cure for your blues."

"Oh?"

"There's an Egyptian exhibit opening up down the road!"

"Oh!" For once, Audra's speechlessness was pleased. "How did I not hear about this?" She scooted closer to the wrought iron table, leaning closer to Jan, heedless of the fact that the metal would dig into her skin.

"Because it hasn't even been announced yet." Jan sipped her tea, leaning forward on the table as well, smiling smugly. "I know the curator of the museum, and he told me about it. The opening

is Saturday, but he agreed to let me bring a friend and walk
through on Friday... since it's going to be our third date."

"You're not fixing me up with someone, are you?"

"No, I figure you'd be too busy staring at all the artifacts to
make decent conversation." Jan tossed her shining brown hair over
her shoulder and smirked at her friend. Audra smiled back,
relieved. "Am I wrong?"

"You know me too well." Audra admitted. "So where is this
place?"

Jan eagerly started talking, only too happy to go on about her
new beau and his job at the local history museum. Audra realized
it was the same place she passed every day on her way to work,
and wondered how she could have missed the squat brick building
with its expansive windows. She supposed it simply had never had
the mystique of Egypt about it before. This exhibit was Jan's
boyfriend's idea, and it was modeled after one that had been
hosted in New York, at the Met. It sounded amazing to Audra, and
she was kind of impressed with Jan's new boyfriend. He actually
sounded like he was far more Audra's type; too bad Jan had found
him first. But then Jan said something that made Audra shiver, and
she interrupted. "I'm sorry, the temple is dedicated to whom?"

"It's one of the lesser-known gods. Brandon calls him some
weird thing, but said I could call him Thoth, since it's easier to
pronounce."

Audra swallowed hard. "Does Brandon say 'Djeuti'?"

"Yes! That's it! I should have known you would know it." Jan
said with a delighted clap of her hands. "He said that the temple
used to be attached to another temple, but it was falling down.
They got permission to move it, since leaving it in the desert
would have guaranteed its destruction."

"I see." Audra sat back and took a long drink of her tea, then
shivered despite the warmth of the day. Jan chattered on, oblivious
to her friend's distraction. After Jan had gone on for a little too
long, they agreed that Audra would meet them at the museum after
dinner, and the girls departed for Audra to return home and Jan

to return to work. Audra checked her kiln, sighing over the drabness of her work, and then swearing aloud when she realized that two of her smaller pieces—one of which was a commission!—had cracked and were ruined. She turned away, fighting tears, wondering where her drive for perfection had gone, where her muse had gone, where her inspiration had gone. She couldn't remember the last time she'd created simply from the fire that had guided her so often in the past.

She couldn't face the ruins of those pots now. She went into the kitchen, grabbed a can of soda and then drifted into her studio to work on some designs for her next paying gig. She'd hoped the change of format to stained glass would give her new inspiration. She flinched away from the reality of it, which was that she'd only taken the job because it would help her pay the rent.

She focused on the work she needed to do to prepare for the class, needing to not think about everything: her lack of creative juice, the gods, *that* god. The exhibit had given her a couple small ideas, and she sketched out a desert scene of a pyramid using reds dark and bright for the sky and sandy golds and yellows for the pyramid itself and the foreground. She sat back and looked at it, and imagined herself in the desert, the gritty sand, the dry heat, the stone. It called to her still, and she sighed and touched the paper wistfully. The dry chalk beneath her fingers mimicked sand enough to give her a hitch in her breath, and she sighed. It was pretty, but it wasn't nearly enough. It was so *ordinary!*

She pushed away from the table irritably and wandered through her house, into her bedroom, which was decorated in the golds and sands of her drawing, with only the dusty red of her bed sheets to relieve the drabness. In the soothing darkness she lay across her bed, the yearning worse than ever, that voice in her head louder now that Jan had brought up Egypt, had said his name aloud. She lolled her head over at her mirror, gazing at the mock-obelisk on her dresser, with its depiction of the Egyptian gods. She'd avoided studying them too closely because every time she heard his name that gravel-and-cream voice came to her, but now it was definitely too late.

She'd once heard a friend who was a writer talk about Thoth, and she'd felt a quiver that had made her blush for days. So naturally she'd avoided him. Wasn't that what any sane person would do, in the presence of something so utterly insane? Who heard voices in their head, after all, but an insane person? *And you,* came the voice. *You are not insane. You wouldn't come to me, so I am here for you.*

She shivered. Now she wasn't going to be able to avoid him any longer. *You're a figment of my imagination.*

Am I? She felt fingers on her body. Touching her thighs, stroking her skin. She shivered. *Figments can do this?*

I must be going crazy. She stood up and walked to the mirror. "I am insane." The obelisk sparkled in the diffuse light. She shook her head. That couldn't be possible. The Thoth figure looked amused. She really was going insane.

Insanity is only expecting a different result from the same action, my dear. You are clearly not insane, since you are questioning everything. Her shirt fluttered as she felt hands sliding up it, even though there was nothing there. Her nipples hardened at the contact. She trembled.

"But you don't exist."

Thousands of people would beg to differ, as would I. The voice in her head was affronted. His hands, however, did not stop massaging her breasts. She bit her lip. *Really, Audra, I didn't expect you to be so stubborn. Didn't you just ask for inspiration?*

She gasped and turned away from the mirror, as if she would see the body behind the hands. The presence chuckled in her head then disappeared. She felt oddly bereft.

The rest of the week passed in a haze from one visitation to another. At first, Thoth made his presence known in small ways—a caress here, a touch there, a breath on her hair—and Audra began looking for him. Then on Thursday he vanished from her side, leaving her convinced she had imagined the entire thing.

Friday came to find her throwing the first work she'd been proud of in a long time. She had taken a design based on an Egyptian-style pot with a long, slender neck, something she didn't think she'd be able to do, a real challenge, and she'd done it! She admired the unfinished product, surprised herself at how well it turned out. She put it into the kiln, saying a small prayer that it would fire properly, and started thinking about designs to paint on it for later. It would fire, it would!

She dressed for the night in jeans with a nice button-down shirt with a green and gold design on it, ate, and drove herself down to the museum. She turned her music up too loud, and left the windows down despite an unexpected chill to the March air. March in Florida did not carry the same weight that it did in the north, but an unexpected cold snap had caused winter to cling to the land like a child to his favorite toy. She ignored the goosebumps, breathing in the air and forcing herself not to think of what she would see, would hear. She tried to listen to the music and not wonder where the voice in her head had gone, why there were no hands on her body, why she felt only anxiety, no hope.

She tried not to reach for the connection, not to look for it, but it was like a sore tooth; impossible to ignore. She turned the radio up louder, drowning out her worries in a storm of music, clashing sound and longing lyrics. She sang along, though she could not have named a single song title after she parked and turned the car off. She approached the museum's doorway and paused, looking around. She had forgotten to ask Jan where they'd be meeting. Just then, a boisterous "hello!" rang out from behind her. She turned, peering into the darkness.

"You must be Audra, Jan's friend. I'm Brandon Gaither, the curator." Audra smiled and took his hand, relieved that Jan's breathless descriptions of him had been hyperbole and not reality. He was cute, but in a bookish, professorial way, not in a supermodel way. She squashed her surprise at Jan allowing him to meet her alone, and did not look around for her friend.

"Hi Brandon, great to meet you." Relieved he didn't try to crush her hand, and delighted with his firm, dry handshake, her smile warmed to a true, friendly one. "Thanks for letting me get the scoop on this exhibit."

"Jan said you were something of an amateur Egyptologist?"

"I don't know if you could call it that. I just dabble. I'm an artist, and a lot of my work takes me to different places for inspiration."

"Ah! So, did you go to school?" She ducked her head at his politeness, and they began the usual small talk between strangers as he escorted her to the back of the museum, the secret entrance that only employees and certain special people saw.

Brandon escorted her to the employees waiting area, where Jan stood, wearing a red sundress that Audra had seen before. She grinned to see it, knowing that Jan called it her 'knockout number,' and crossed to hug her friend.

"You made it!"

"I wouldn't miss this!" They exchanged greetings, knowing glances, and Audra complimented Jan on her outfit. After a moment of girlish chatter, Jan took Audra's arm and pulled her towards the door, where Brandon stood, shifting from foot to foot.

"Come on, I know Brandon is dying to show you the big pieces!"

"We are fortunate enough to have a piece from the Valley of the Kings," he said, puffing his chest out. "Nothing so grand as from Tut's tomb or anything, but it's still gold."

He led the way to the Egyptian exhibit, pointing out artwork in the main galley, discussing the historical ramifications of this sculpture and that painting. Audra could see Jan's interest was feigned, but the simple fact that her friend covered the boredom left no doubt that she really liked this guy. They arrived at the beginning of the Egyptian section, and Audra no longer cared about Jan's interest, since her own was genuine. She oohed and ahhed over the cases full of tiny artifacts, larger jewelry, and the promised piece of gold—a glorious burial necklace from some grand tomb. The scarab in the center was nearly as large as Audra's palm, and she stared at it, entranced, as Brandon spoke of a cartouche on the back of the scarab proclaiming which king had worn it.

She didn't notice, at first, the *other presence* behind her, because she found herself hurrying to catch up to Brandon and Jan as they began to wander off while she studied each item. At a statue of Anubis, while she crouched to study the hieroglyphics on the base she belatedly realized she couldn't even hear them, yet she didn't feel alone.

And so you are not alone. The feeling of rough fingertips brushing along her face accompanied the voice. She jumped, standing. *I do wish you'd worn a skirt.* Hands sliding across her ass. She backed up against the statue. *Oh, no. I do believe you are in the wrong place.* She felt the hands again, beneath her back and legs, and gasped as she was lifted. She splayed her hands, flailing a bit, and touched, then wrapped her arms around a solid body. For a moment she caught a glimpse of dark skin and darker eyes, and she reeled from the impact of that gaze upon hers.

"You are real," she breathed, her heart pounding.

Why must you see things to believe in them? The voice in her head was exasperated. She felt a giggle bubbling in her throat, but she feared giving voice to it, feared it would lead to laughter that would have Jan and Brandon asking how it was she floated through the museum... and it occurred to her to wonder, as she glanced around, where her friends were, and how he knew his way around so well.

"Where are Jan and Brandon... and where are we going?"

"Your friends are otherwise occupied. And I'm taking you to my corner of your world." She gasped as she heard the voice echoing off the walls around her, as the man holding her became more and more visible to the eye. She stared at his face, at his profile. His full lips begged to be kissed, even as the harsh set of his mouth made her nervous. She released him, pushing back a bit. He turned his head to hers, his eyes full of dark promises. "I am not going to hurt you, Audra." Hearing her name pass his lips made her heart do flips, and she licked her lips. "I will not force you. All you need do is say no, and I will disappear into the night, never to trouble you again." She relaxed; the press of his skin warmed her. "But say yes, and I shall show you the gifts you should have, the things you have been missing, the creative energy you have begged for." His eyes darkened. "And I will show you how a woman should be pleasured." She swallowed, her eyes flickering from his to try and find a safe place to land. She could not escape his presence; his hands cradled her, the kyphi scent of him swirled about her, the dizzying gift of knowledge he'd just given her thrilled through her. She wondered if this was how Eve had felt when she'd bitten into the apple. She wet her lips and tried to think of a good reason to say no, but the simple fact of the matter remained: She wanted her creativity back, and she wanted this being, this god to make love to her. Those desires outweighed any argument she could have made for the other side. She lifted her gaze back to his fathomless eyes and leaned towards him. He shook his head slightly. "In this, my dear, you must speak your heart."

A lump filled her throat, and she gasped softly. Saying aloud that she needed to find her creative self would be easy, but to speak aloud that she wanted to feel like a woman, to feel sexy, could she bring herself to do that? She flushed and closed her eyes. "I want to find my creative spirit again, to know that spark I've been lacking."

She felt him shift, and they were walking again. She opened her eyes, and they stood before a temple. The temple, *his* temple. She had not expected it to be so large, or to be in such an open space. It was not square, not exactly. It had a long, narrow entrance that vanished into darkness, and the entire thing reminded her of a square bottle. The sandy stone held a bit of an orange tinge, except on the right side, which clearly had been built by modern hands. She let her head fall back against his shoulder as she looked up. The ceiling was clear glass, and the stars shone in the sky above. The lighting in the room glowed only enough to guide you to the doorway, which lurked there to admit those brave enough to pass through it. He set her down, and she looked up at him. He was solid, now, and she could see all of him as he stepped closer to the temple. He wore only an Egyptian-style linen kilt, baring his broad chest, arms, and strong calves to her greedy eyes. She found herself almost disappointed he wasn't wearing the crown he so often wore in hieroglyphics, or any other incredible jewels. She tried to imagine them as he folded his arms and looked at her, waiting. "Was there nothing else, Audra?"

She flushed as he began walking away, towards the dim interior temple. She watched him go, wondering if he would leave her. The thought spurred her into calling "Wait!" He turned slowly, looking at her with an expectant light in his eyes. "Yes, there's something else. I want you." He waited. She blushed, feeling her cheeks burn. "I want you to show me what you promised." He lifted his eyebrows, and she lowered her voice to a whisper, finally finding the word she'd been looking for. "To ravish me."

"Then come, enter the chamber of mystery." He backed to the doorway. "And become the mystery."

She could not stop blushing, but she forced her feet forward, at first slowly, then darting into his arms. He swept her into a kiss that literally took her off her feet for a moment as he lifted her and pressed her into the wall behind her. With the cool stone behind her, the warm, incredible, impossible body before her, and the heat of his kiss, Audra thought she would faint, or perhaps swoon, like one of those characters in one of the old romances her grandmother used to read. Then he was licking her throat, and she let her head fall to one side to give him better access, and while she could still think, she had one final thought that made her gasp and speak fearfully. "But what about Jan—"

"They will not disturb us." His words carried some finality, some ring of command that she could not argue with. Instead she moaned as he nibbled on her neck, his hands sliding over her hips, up her ribcage, cupping her breasts, his thumbs rubbing her nipples. A frenzy of need gripped her and she reached for him, wanting to feel his skin, to touch him, to reassure herself that this was really not some elaborate hoax her brain was playing on her. He chuckled softly and took her hands, kissing each. His lips were so soft against her fingertips. Then, with a swift movement that widened her eyes and pulled a gasp from her lips, he pressed her arms above her head. Her body arched out, pressing against his, and she squirmed as she realized how much of her was now pressed against him—and felt the length and heat of his hard cock for the first time.

"Thoth—"

"You know, that is not truly my name," he purred, his voice a rumble that carried into her chest, making her nipples peak and sending a streak of heat into her groin. He nuzzled her neck, sliding his hands down her arms, pressing them into the wall. The command was implicit; she stayed still, linking her fingers together.

"Djeuti," she whispered.

"Yes," he said, his tone smug. "Good girl." He slid his hand down her hair, caressing her cheek. "In this temple, I will be your Master." He nuzzled her ear, his breath warm. "Your body will be mine." She shivered with delight and a frisson of fear. He licked then bit her earlobe before nipping down her neck, lightly at first then harder, making her whimper and squirm against him. Just when she thought she would break, would need to touch him, he stopped. She made a sound of protest, and he chuckled softly. "There is plenty of time, my dear."

He slid his hands down her body, molding it, pulling her shirt up. The air was cool on her skin, making it prickle with gooseflesh. He skimmed his fingertips up, under her shirt, over her stomach. She fought back a giggle. His fingers barely brushed the lace of her bra, seeking her hard nipples to tease and torment. The giggle became a soft gasp. He slid his hands to cup her breasts through the bra, thumb rubbing across her nipple as he kissed her again. Their tongues swirled and caressed, and she felt as though she were melting into him. Her arms slid down the wall as her body opened to his, growing heavy with passion. He allowed his hands to glide down her body, stroking her skin, awakening every nerve. He cupped her ass, pressing her closer to him, then lifted her. She wrapped her legs around him, blushing, feeling like a teenager again, dry-humping in a museum. She buried her face in his shoulder, kissing his neck, her hands tracing his back.

"Look at me," he murmured against her ear, grinding against her. She whimpered, her body responding, so heavy and full, nerve endings on fire. She leaned back, looking into his eyes, her own heavy-lidded. "I want to see you when you come." She blushed and looked away. He lifted one hand to her face, cupping her chin, turning her towards him. He spoke softly, huskily, but with a sexy edge. "Let me see you."

She could not deny him. Her hips moved in rhythm with his already; she couldn't imagine how much better it would be without clothing. He kissed her again, then pulled back, staring into her eyes. His cock was so hot and hard against her, she could not stop writhing. He watched her, his hands skimming her back, sliding around to cup her breasts, holding her close. He whispered so softly she could not make out what he was saying. Finally, it did not matter. She came, throwing her head back, crying out, and shuddering in his arms, while he held her close. She quivered with aftershocks for several moments; he simply stroked her hair and let her recover.

She had no words, instead kissed him deeply. He tangled his hand in her hair and thrust his tongue in her mouth. She moaned and tightened her legs around him. When he broke the kiss they were both panting. He let her down gently and stepped back.

He gestured down the hall, towards the shadowed entrance of the temple. "Shall we?" She smiled. He took that as assent, smiled back and began walking backwards, unwrapping his kilt. Before she could see anything, he was lost to the shadows. She pushed off the wall and gathered herself, first taking her shoes and socks off, leaving them at the outermost entrance before slowly pacing down the barely-lit hall. She unbuttoned her shirt as she walked, peeling it off and discarding it in the slender passageway. She reached the sanctuary to find Thoth standing, nude, in the center of it. She paused to stare. He was magnificent, his entire body hard, limned in the darkness like an eclipse. He smiled at her. She smiled back and knelt.

"I am yours," she said softly.

"Yes." His voice was a whisper, but it seemed to shake her, to pierce her to her heart, as though she had heard it with more than just her ears. Then his hands were in her hair, his lips on hers, and she fell back on the sand and stone and linen beneath her. Thoth was heat and skin and sweat above her. He kissed and licked his way down her body, starting with her collarbone, teasingly slow. Her hands caressed his back and up his neck, onto the unfamiliar planes of his smooth, shaved head. His dark skin made hers seem luminous in the soft light, and she moaned as he slipped her bra down and took a peaked nipple into his mouth. He skimmed his hand across her skin, squeezing the other breast, pinching that nipple, then pulling both as he suckled. She arched against him, spreading her legs and pressing herself into his body. He growled approvingly.

"Oh, yes," she whispered, as he slid lower, licking her breast and then skipping the lace of her bra to nip at her stomach. She curled up to unhook her bra and toss it aside. He licked the underside of each breast, swirling his way down, pausing to wait for her to unhook her pants and wriggle out of them. He tossed them aside, then began nibbling at her leg, starting at the knee. He pressed little, tender bites near her knee, then abruptly slid down near her panties and bit her inner thigh hard. She gasped, but the sensation was too intense for pain, too sharp for simply pleasure. She could not bring herself to slither away or arch into it, and then he bit her other thigh, a gentler bite, swirling his tongue around and sucking on the flesh. Pleasure gathered, growing, a heaviness in her arms as she reached for him to pull him closer. He gripped her wrists, shaking his head.

"I am Master here," he purred softly. He pressed her hands down, then pulled her panties off. She flushed with more than pleasure, fighting the urge to hide her face as he spread her legs. Surely he was a god, he'd seen it all, right? She closed her eyes. "Audra." She tried to pretend she hadn't heard him. "Audra." Sharp edges to his voice this time. She opened her eyes. "Never forget you are beauty itself, always."

"I..." She could not finish her thought. He had lowered his head, and swept away all thoughts with a caress of his hands across her thighs, a sweep of his tongue across her pussy. He didn't attack, like some of her lovers had, or act as if he were simply there as a favor to her. He laved, his tongue glided from one end of her pussy lips all the way to her clit, and then he sucked it with a delicacy that had her crying out in shock and pleasure from the orgasm that crested so quickly she had no chance to try and hold on to it, to draw it out. He gave her no chance to recover, his lips and tongue drove her on until all she could do was make tiny mewling noises in the back of her throat, pleading for release.

He stopped, pulling a cry of distress from her, as he crawled up her body, pausing to bite each nipple gently, making her writhe against him. "Please," she gasped, as he shifted so that his cock pressed against her clit, pinning it between them.

He rose above her, kissing her deeply, and she risked his wrath, clinging to him, wrapping her arms and legs around him as if she would merge with him. He growled, breaking the kiss and taking her hands to pin them to the floor. "Submit," he whispered.

"I said I was yours," she said, writhing against him.

"Submit." He said, his voice thrumming. She shivered, stilling, her eyes meeting his.

"Yes," she said.

He kissed her, and she opened her mouth to him. As his tongue tenderly swirled around hers, he slid his cock over her clit, making her moan, and finally plunged into her body. She shuddered, breaking the kiss to gasp in air. The tension between them built, and she arched into his thrusts. She moaned as his hand skimmed over her skin, finding her breast and cupping, caressing. Audra fell into the pleasure, letting it carry her. She closed her eyes, tilting her head back, baring her throat to him.

He lifted her hips, pulling her onto his cock, pounding into her, and she gasped as his thumb found her clit, rubbing. Her orgasm stalked closer, and she whimpered, waiting for it to pounce, wanting it to make that final leap.

He moaned, and his thrusts slowed but increased in force, slamming into her. She arched back, reaching for him, unable to stop herself, clawing at his thighs. Just then, her orgasm finally leaped, sinking its teeth into her, shaking her, and she shuddered beneath him, her body spasming around his, and she panted with pleasure. He bared his teeth in a snarl of pleasure and pounded her a few more times before releasing a howl of pleasure as he climaxed.

He fell forward onto her, and she held him for a long moment, their breathing the only sound echoing in the sacred chamber. He pulled back, kissed her gently, and smiled.

"I'll never lack for inspiration again," she said with a wry chuckle.

"I am so very glad."

"There you are!" Jan said, glaring at Audra. "I was so worried!"

"I'm fine. It's not like I could get lost." Audra brushed a lock of stray hair out of her face and gave Jan a confused frown. "Where would I go?"

"Well..." Jan stared at Audra, looking between her and Brandon, completely confused. "I suppose you're right. But... don't do that again, OK?"

"Jan. I'm a big girl. I'll do what I want. Let's go finish looking around, shall we?" Audra strode off, heading away from the temple, leaving a very confounded Jan in her wake.

Ordinary Girl
M.A. Earnshaw

She was average, indistinct. The people passing by barely gave her a glance, the girl entirely too ordinary to warrant much attention.

But the second glance was guaranteed. Every one of us looked twice.

The realization was like waking from a dream, hazy and soft, into the bright arms of the morning. It was too sharp, too insistent, but once you were awake there was no going back. No one else questioned why they were drawn to look again, their eyes lingering on mousy hair and quiet eyes and small frame, but once I'd seen it, I couldn't stop looking.

Actually, it was less about seeing it and more about feeling it. When you got close it was like there was a current crackling through the air around her, gentler than magnetism but still enough to raise the hairs on your body and too powerful to resist.

Perhaps it was just because I had nobody with me, nothing else to focus on other than the roadies uncoiling cables and lugging speaker cabinets across the stage. The only thing vying for my attention was the faint thump thump thump of the songs playing over the PA system. I'd bought two tickets to the gig originally, safe in the knowledge that I'd be coming with my man, but too late I'd found myself with a spare ticket, an empty bed, and a lack of friends to accompany me in this new city. Rather than face another night in the apartment alone I'd decided to come anyway. Maybe, I'd thought, I could meet some like-minded people—except that wasn't working out so well because everyone else was already with someone, friends and lovers sharing easy laughs and embraces as they waited for the show to begin.

The only other person on their own here was that girl, and she didn't look starving for company. She held herself too high, and the smile she wore was satisfied, relaxed. For whatever reason she had ended up here alone, she wasn't feeling self-conscious about it. Not like me.

I was on the edge of the crowd, out of the way to stop myself being buffeted by all the movement, and it was easy to lean against a pillar and watch her. More interestingly, watch people's reactions to her. The head snap as they walked by and *had* to look back at her. The faltered footsteps as they approached her, momentarily distracted from their forward motion by the mere sight of her. The spilt drinks as groups of friends stumbled into each other as they slowed to take that second glance.

And there was nothing, nothing at all to explain why.

For the first time her gaze left the movement on the stage and swept to meet mine, her expression inscrutable from across the room, but I looked away anyway. It was rude to be caught staring, even if I wasn't the only person doing it. By the time I chanced another glance in her direction, she was gone.

The heat had crept up with the increased press of bodies, and I licked my dry lips, leaving my spot to seek the bar at the back of the room. I only wanted water to ease the thirst, but the bartender didn't seem to hear me over the commotion of the room and poured me a beer anyway.

"I'll have the same," a voice said beside me, and I knew without looking who it belonged to. It was as ordinary as the rest of her, a mezzo-soprano, softly confident, and yet the physical reaction it caused in my body was anything but ordinary. The whispers in my head, the warning bells that my primitive side was ringing, erupted in a harsh cacophony, but my pulse and my body reacted in ways that only hours of foreplay had ever managed to achieve before now—a tight ache that began in my breasts, coiled in my belly and finished between my legs, slick and ready.

I didn't look, even after paying for the beer and chugging

half of it down. I simply watched the slight, pale hand curl around the plastic cup on the bar next to mine and trace the beads of condensation with a finger.

"I saw you watching me," she said, and this time I couldn't not look.

She was every bit as plain up close, down to her freckled nose and grey eyes. And still my body sang louder.

"Doesn't everybody?" The beer seemed to be hitting me quickly, the world around me already growing fuzzy around the edges.

"You noticed that?" Her face was just as inexpressive, but if there was any emotion I'd have been able to name, it was a note of surprise in her voice. I couldn't answer, finishing the beer and signaling the bartender for another. I needed the alcohol to calm my warring instincts.

The stage erupted into life behind us, a tumble of light and sound, spotlights reflecting off the chrome of the bar. Drumbeats echoed around the theatre and up through the soles of my feet, an answering pulse to my own.

"Want to dance?" Her breath was hot against my neck.

She held her hand out, steady and certain. I glanced between that hand and the black swarm of the crowd, turning back to down the beer and take her hand.

Her skin was cool, far too cool against mine, and she pulled me into the melee, right into the centre of the swarm, where the bodies around us crushed us together. She took advantage of the necessary closeness, looping her arms around my hips and pulling them into hers, hands resting lightly just above the swell of my buttocks. I didn't know what to do with mine; they found her waist.

Our hips moved in sync, no space to move our feet, lips bare inches away. I was just slightly taller than her, which was disconcerting. I'd only ever danced with people taller than me before, at least as intimately as this. I'd always been sure of my sexuality and my desire for men, but my body seemed to be eager for this change, even if my head was still playing catch-up.

"I've never done this before." The words spilled out, and even I wasn't sure what I meant, but she smiled like she knew.

"That's not a problem."

She led the movement because I couldn't. My head was spinning from the beer, from the heat, from the throb between my legs. She was so close and I was submerged in wide, black pupils, vaguely aware that despite the heat, despite the sweat I could feel beading on my own skin, her face was free of perspiration or the flush of heat. The warning bells jangled again, but their sound was so much quieter than the thud of the band and the pulse of my arousal. It was easy to ignore them.

I couldn't distinguish between songs, the world around me gaining the consistency of cotton candy and when I felt fresh night air, the chill was welcome and refreshing. I could still hear the band playing inside, but for some reason we were outside, our hands clasped, and a taxi was pulling up in front of us.

I didn't even know her name.

She encouraged me to give the driver my address, and as soon as the words had been delivered, her mouth was on mine, lips and tongue demanding. I didn't have the presence of mind to wonder about the show we were giving to the driver. She kept tight hold of both my hands, resting them in our laps, our fingers the only parts of our bodies that were touching other than our mouths. The only part of my body that I could really *feel* now, sensation centered on the sweep of her tongue and the pressure of her lips. I'd never been kissed like this before. Never knew I *could* be kissed like this.

The driver was tipped well and I unlocked the door with shaky hands, dropping the keys to the hall carpet as she deadlocked the door behind us. I forgot the keys, forgot to even reach for the light switch, leaving us illuminated only by the pale light from the street outside, hesitantly filtering through the blinds.

I didn't need to see anything anyway, other than the gleam of her teeth as she smiled. I couldn't see her eyes, couldn't see the intent of that smile, but I'd drowned the warning bells out so well now that I couldn't hear them at all anymore.

"Bedroom?" she asked, and I took her hand as I had at the bar, leading her the few steps to the door, over the threshold.

This time I did try to reach for the light switch but her hand was there first, her fingers twining with mine as she pushed me towards the bed. The room was brighter than the hallway and her hair was cast with strange amber tones in the glow from the streetlamps, her skin warmer, her eyes even colder in the dark. My cheeks were burning again, and her cool fingertips brushed over them, before cupping behind my neck and guiding my face to hers. I wasn't as hesitant this time—not as passive, fighting back against her dominance—and I could feel her delighted grin against my lips.

We bumped into my dresser and she released me, hands reaching to strip herself of clothes in simple, practiced movements, until she was bare in front of me, fingers sliding under the hem of my t-shirt and trailing a cold path up my spine.

"This all needs to come off," she said, demanding, and I faltered again.

"I've never done this," I repeated my words from earlier. "I've never—not with a woman."

There was a hint of impatience in her next words. "You'll know."

She tugged at the shirt and I let her pull it from me, bra following, and I pushed through my nerves to undo my jeans, kicking them free of my feet when I was done. I wasn't as casual about my nudity as she was. The things that I had done before had always been under the cover of blankets or true darkness, away from scrutiny and judgment. But she wasn't judging me.

She reached for me, pulling me close so we were hip to hip, just as we had been earlier as we danced. Except our breasts brushed together, and I could feel the movement of her belly against mine as we breathed, and all of that soft, cool skin was pressed up against me.

Her mouth moved down my neck, hands stroking my butt, her teeth finding the tenderest spot on my collarbone until I cried out, knees threatening to give way, leaning into her body for support. She pushed me backwards again until I hit the stool in front of the dresser, and I sprawled over it. I could see the triumph in her fresh smile, and in the next moment she was on her knees, pushing my legs apart.

One hand brushed against my inner thigh, higher and higher until it was just at the spot where leg became more, but there it stayed, thumb stroking the crease while I writhed, bent backwards and unable to right myself the way I was lying. I felt her lips against my ankle, teasing a trail up my calf until she found the back of my knee, wrapping my leg over her shoulder so she had access to it with tongue and teeth.

I didn't understand how kissing me there could magnify the ache between my legs, or cause the coiling in my belly to tighten, but it did. I lifted a trembling hand to her head, twisting my fingers into her hair to tug it higher, desperate to see if she could be everything she promised. She still took her time, exploring the sensitive skin of my thigh, and when I reached in impatience to stroke myself, she slapped my hand away, nipping along my thigh with her teeth. I whimpered, hips thrusting off the stool and against the empty air, seeking whatever friction I could get.

She didn't tease me much longer, mouth descending to where I was wet and waiting.

I could feel the movement of her lips and tongue against me in every nerve my body possessed, every caress of her mouth causing my back to arch and the breath to leave my lungs in a shattered gasp. She kept her movements slow, gentle, letting the fire inside me simmer and crackle, until I was begging for her to let it go, let it consume me.

"Please, please -" I could hear myself chanting, and she ignored my mantra, going ever softer. Just as the fire flared, on the verge of burning me whole, she pulled away.

I gasped, reaching for her blindly, but she was already on her feet, grasping my hands and pulling me upright in one swift movement. Her strength in that moment didn't really register over the throb of my body, angry at being denied satisfaction when we'd been so close. She spun me so I was at the foot of the bed, pushing me down until I was bent, ass in the air, and I felt the sharp sting of a slap on the flesh there. I cried out again, the sound cut off in a moan as she massaged the skin, and she bent over me, so I could feel the electric thrill of her skin pressed against my back.

"Why should you have all the fun?" she whispered.

We rolled until we were side by side, legs tangled, and when she kissed me I could taste myself on her. I knew what she wanted from me, what her words had meant, and let my fingers trace a path from her waist, down over her hip, to the bare skin of her sex. I touched her as I would want to be touched, tentative and tender, but she grasped my hand, increasing the pressure and guiding me, hips rolling against the movement of my fingers.

And she was touching me again, avoiding my clit and instead exploring every other part of me, fingers gliding over my aching skin before pressing into me. I knew why she wasn't touching me where I wanted it the most; it would take nothing to push me over the edge. I tried to ignore the insistent conflagration inside me and focus on pleasing her, watching her face to learn what brought her close.

It became so hard though, every limb trembling with the difficulty of holding back when I wanted to let go. My mantra had returned, only this time I was begging her to find her release so I would know I hadn't failed her.

"Please," I gasped, my mouth against her breast, "I want…"

She rolled us again so she was above me.

"Do you trust me?"

It was an unfair question. The answer couldn't ever really be yes, not if I were to mean it, but she knew that I could only ever answer with 'yes' in this moment.

Her thumb brushed close, and I twisted my hips to try and meet it, and she bit at the skin of my neck to remind me that I had to answer if I wanted release.

"Y—yes."

I was suddenly aware of the forceful rush of energy through my body, a fierce sensation that burned my skin inwards, flames licking to meet the spiral of pleasure in my center, the fire reflected in her eyes as I stared up at her. Her lips met mine for the last time, thumb finally touching me where I needed it, and I was done, shattering outwards in infinite shards of light.

Even as my splintered fragments floated somewhere not on earth, I could still feel her, connected to me, taking from me. Her mouth was still on mine and I was giving to her, the pull coming from my belly; I could feel it almost like a cord connected to her. This was what she'd sought from me all along.

I should have struggled against her feeding from me—because that's exactly what it was—but it was prolonging the sweet rush of release and I could only surrender to it.

Then I was back in my body, limp on the bed, trying to focus on the ceiling above me. Exhaustion didn't come close to describing the intense lethargy settling into my bones; I was barely able to keep my grip on the thread of consciousness.

She rested on her elbows beside me, the picture of satiation. The amber glow was sharper around her, and it wasn't from the streetlamps at all; it was all her. All I could think of when I looked at her, blinking back my heavy eyelids, was a cat lazing in the sunshine. Even in repose the inhuman grace in her body was obvious, no linger hidden by the subterfuge she'd worn in public.

It took a long time to gather the fragments of my thoughts together well enough to speak.

"What are you?" I pulled the bedcovers around my body like they could shield me from anger, if that's where the question led her.

"Succubus," she replied, stretching out so her hips rolled gracefully against the mattress. She looked entirely unconcerned by my curiosity, but that didn't stop the spike of fear that found its way to my throat. I'd felt the strength in her.

It couldn't be a good thing that she'd confessed so readily— and to being something that didn't even exist. Except she did exist. And I knew her words were true.

"Are you going to kill me?" The words weren't even a whisper, barely formed against my tongue.

"Why call attention to myself? Most people don't even remember that I've been with them. I'm not happy that you will remember, but you won't tell anyone. Who could you even tell?"

She was right, of course. I had no one, and there wasn't a person in the world who would believe me even if I did.

"So you'll just...leave?"

It seemed too easy, too neat. Too normal an ending.

"I'll be gone by morning, yes. Staying around would be no good for you—that's a certain way to kill you. You can only feed me so much before I take too much and leave nothing for you."

"Why could I see you?" I whispered, fighting the fatigue. "Why could I tell?"

"Who knows? You weren't the first." She was utterly disinterested. "You should sleep. Try to forget about me."

And I did succumb to sleep, an empty void of time without dreams, and when morning broke in soft golden light, I was alone in the bed again, like every morning.

But I hadn't forgotten. I would never forget.

The Warmth of a Wood Nymph
Clarice Clique

Tatyanah smiled down at the naked man kneeling in front of her. It was a smile filled with promise, but the man couldn't see it or the undisguised lust in the woman's eyes, his gaze was focused on the hard stone floor.

"Are you certain of your vow to pledge your life to me as your Princess?" Tatyanah said walking slowly round the man's body. "It is not too late to change your mind. I can still order my mother to return you to whatever barbarian land spawned you."

Her words caused him something akin to physical pain. They both knew that it was far too late.

"I pledge you my life. My spirit and soul are yours. Every last drop of blood in my body belongs to you." His voice possessed a deep timbre which reflected all the power of his muscular body. Tatyanah had decided long ago to allow him to retain the remnants of his rough tribal accent and had never regretted it.

The princess silently nodded and for a moment her smile was replaced with a more serious expression. She picked up a brush from her dressing table and pulled it once through the length of her auburn hair. Then she began to slowly circle him. The heels of her shoes clicked on the floor, it was the only audible sound in her bedchamber. Then with a sudden sharp movement she brought the back of the hairbrush down hard on his exposed buttocks.

He gasped as the hard wood slapped against his defenseless skin. He tried to suppress his cries as the wood thwacked against him for a second, third, fourth time. By the twentieth time he had lost count, he was digging his nails into the palm of the hand, desperately trying to maintain control of himself.

"I ask you again, are you certain you are willing to pledge your life to serve your Princess?" She spoke the words as hard staccato sounds between the spanks. "Are you willing to obey my every command without ever questioning or doubting me?"

"I am, Princess."

She hit him with all her strength and then returned the brush to her dressing table. He didn't breathe until she returned to his side and her hand gently caressed the crevice between his buttocks.

"Your flesh has such a beautiful sheen to it now, my sweet little pet; would you like to see it?"

It wasn't a question he was expected to answer. Tatyanah grabbed a handful of his hair and pulled him in front of her mirrors. She had had them positioned to allow him to see the rear of his body and now he gazed in silence at the red shine she had given his tanned skin. She spread his buttocks and played her fingers round the creases of his revealed hole.

"Shall I fuck you today? Do you think you deserve to be fucked?" Her voice was the same one she used when she met foreign dignitaries and ambassadors.

"I never deserve to receive any reward from you, my Princess. It is your boundless grace that keeps me in your presence, not my worthiness."

Tatyanah laughed. "You are the most amusing toy I've ever possessed."

He waited for her to order him to fetch the phallic object she kept in her wardrobe and strap it around her waist, or for her to lie back on her bed and give him the rare order to penetrate her, but she didn't say anything.

Finally, she sighed heavily, and a warning sensation pricked across his skin.

"Dear darling, little pet, I am truly fond of you, but if you wish to serve me, if you wish me to retain you as my favorite pet then you have to do more."

His whole body tensed.

"I want to see a real cock fucking your cute little bottom. I think we need something special."

There was a pause as if she was thinking, but he knew her now, everything with her was carefully planned, nothing was ever spontaneous, however she made it appear.

"We need something special," she said. "The first time a male penetrates you will be a unique experience, it must be done properly. I think what we need is the creature of lust. A wood nymph." Then her voice changed from slow consideration to snapped commands. "Go into the forest, capture one of those wood nymphs, and bring it back to me before moonrise."

He dared to look at her. She did not rebuke him, or tell him to fetch one of the many articles she used to punish him; instead she remained laying on the bed, smiling at him, her green eyes as hard as the most precious stone. In movements so small and measured that another man wouldn't have seen them at all, her fingers began to pull the material of her skirt to reveal her naked skin. He waited, unaware of the aching in his muscles, as the fabric traveled with painful slowness up her legs. When the hem had allowed his eyes to newly discover the pale flesh of her thighs and was on the edge of unveiling her secret haven, her smile widened.

"I have given you an order," she said.

"Thank you, my Princess," he said.

He raised himself off the floor in one smooth movement and bowed low to the woman, too aware of the hardness of his manhood pressing into the tight muscles of his stomach.

He looked around him. All he saw was trees and more trees. He had a sudden deep yearning for the faraway deserts of his homeland. As a youngster he had thought that sand covered the whole world, he'd plagued the returning hunting expeditions with questions of what they'd seen, barely believing their answers. And now he was forced to believe it, surrounded by greenery for the rest of his foreseeable life, never likely to see a single grain of sand again. And he was the lucky one. The rest of his party had been mercilessly slain. There had hardly been time to defend themselves. He was lucky the Princess had been there, had seen him and had seen something in him she wanted. And it had been his fault. He had wanted to venture further, see new lands; he had pushed his men further than they wanted to go, further than they had felt safe. Further than they had been safe. He had wanted his father to be proud of him. And now here he was, the oldest son of the king, separated eternally from his own people. He knew that he didn't deserve to be under Tatyanah's protection. He didn't deserve to be her favorite pet. But he was. He was lucky.

He chose the direction opposite to the rising sun and walked on with a purpose. He did not know what a wood nymph was or how he was supposed to capture one, but if she had wanted him to know she would have told him, his ignorance was all part of her game. She enjoyed testing him; she knew he would always do everything in his power to serve his Princess. Even though he wasn't certain what his power was anymore. He had been a great warrior, he had had the three most beautiful known women as his wives, and he had been a respected leader. A respected man. But over the time he'd been with her he'd quickly learnt that the Princess responded with the most pleasure when he did unmanly things. She'd had her loudest orgasm pleasuring herself after she made him cry for the first time.

Thinking of his Princess gave him the familiar warmth in his groin. He thought of the latest order she had given him, the confidence and assurance that radiated from her when she told him she wanted to see him fucked by a man, and his cock hardened. He looked down at himself, yearning to touch the part of him that was reaching out for attention. But one of the first rules Tatyanah had given him was to forbid him to touch himself without her permission. She hadn't given him permission for a long time. His hand almost began to move of its own accord, but he managed to force it to stay by his side. Then a treacherous thought began to creep into his mind that she would never know what he did out here on his own. He imagined how good it would feel to relieve himself. He could visualize his hand on his cock. Then he closed his eyes and he could see his Princess's hand on his cock.

A twig snapped behind him, instinctively he fell to his knees. He had been about to betray his Princess, and she had foreseen he would betray her and had followed him knowing what she would catch him doing.

A merry laugh tinkled around him. It wasn't the Princess, but it was certain to be another of her pets she had sent to spy on him. It was giving himself far too much importance to believe for a moment that the Princess would think he was worth the effort for her to follow him herself.

"I am a loyal subject of the Princess Tatyanah until the last breath escapes my body," he said, certain that death was upon him, that the princess had sent him out here to have him disposed of out of her sight and care.

The laughter continued. "I don't give a piss for your princess Tatyanah, but you might be of more interest. Stand up and let me see you properly."

He was so accustomed to obeying orders that he immediately stood up even as he felt an emotion rising in him that he was no longer accustomed to, an anger at the insult given to his Princess in this creature's lack of proper respect.

"I like what I see so far. Now turn around to face me so I can see everything you have to offer."

He turned, grateful to have an opportunity to see the only person he'd encountered who hadn't given his Princess the reverence she naturally warranted, to see the man who might be his enemy. He found himself gazing at a man's chest. The flesh was as pale as that of all the people of this country, but the man had strangely dark nipples, which were standing erect from his white skin. He forced his eyes to travel up a long neck, over full, dark, berry-shaded lips which were slightly parted in a teasing smile, over a noble shaped nose, to meet the other man's gaze. There was an unusual glint in the man's eyes, which were of a color closer to silver than any other known hue. He felt dizzy looking at him; it was as if he was staring at the sun, but he was determined not to look away and show weakness in front of someone who had not respected his Princess. The longer he looked the more his head hurt, the pain inside his skull grew like a creature getting endlessly bigger through clawing and biting and feeding on his brain.

Finally the other man laughed throwing his head back. "You like pain, do you, my friend?"

He hardly heard the words; he had been focusing all the power in his body in continuing to meet the silver eyed gaze. Now it was broken, he felt like he was falling and couldn't support his own weight. As his mind began to clear he realized he would have fallen to the ground, but the other man had stepped forward and had put his arms around his waist to support him. He became aware of his skin pressed against the other man's. The other man's body was cold but somehow his touch made him feel warm, where his long fingers were stretched across the small of his back he felt a heat that was spreading outwards and encompassing the whole of his being. Then he had a consciousness that his manhood was brushing against this man's leg, was more than brushing, it was rising, stretching, wanting to push against this other being, to bury itself into the heat.

He pulled backwards away from the silver eyed man's touch; he stared at the brown ground, clenched his fist, and tried to prepare himself for facing the other man again. When he looked up, though, he couldn't force himself to meet the unreadable gaze of those strange eyes; instead he tried to focus on another part of his body. He searched the face, the sharp cheekbones, the high forehead; for a moment his gaze settled on the man's hair, which was longer and fairer than any he had seen on a male before, but his eyes couldn't settle. He looked at the lithe body, which seemed too slender to have supported his own muscular frame. Then his eyes stopped. Between those long legs, his eyes stopped. It was as if his vision was trapped, more so than when he had been looking into his eyes. He didn't know why he couldn't look away. The man was larger than any he had seen before, but he was just a man, like any other man he'd seen any other time. But this was different. He had never been alone in the presence of another naked man, a fully aroused man, and staring at the man's excited state was making his own manhood mirror the stranger's.

"Who are you?" he said, trying to compose himself, pulling

his eyes up to the man's flat stomach. He wished for the first time that he was more than his Princess's pet, that he had high enough rank to at least have a piece of cloth to cover his groin from the dancing eyes of this other man. But, no, he was proud the beautiful Princess had chosen him, had saved his pitiful life. He must strive to act now in a manner that would make her proud of him. He raised his eyes to the other man's face and spoke again, louder and more determined. "I can see you are a slave like me, so why do you dare to be so bold and use the Princess's name so impudently?"

The man's lips curled into a small smile. "Tell me how you can see I am a slave." His voice wasn't as harsh as the Princess's, but it was definitely mocking him just as she did.

"You are not deemed worthy to wear any clothes. You are entirely naked as I am."

"As you are indeed." The silver eyed man reached a hand out as if he was going to caress his skin, but he stopped his hand a breath away from touching him and merely smiled at him before folding his fingers up and returning them to rest on his own body.

"Do you like that I am naked?"

The words were a clear tease and the other man began to dance the tips of his fingers over his hard nipples with a smile on his face that looked as if any moment it would turn, break open and release loud peals of laughter.

"I answered your question, show honour and answer mine. Who are you?"

"If you want to know me, I want to know you."

He swallowed hard, even though he was avoiding the gaze of the silver eyes, he could feel the other man staring at him and he wasn't sure if he had understood what the man had said correctly or incorrectly.

"I am a loyal slave of Princess Tatyanah until the last..."

"I have heard that already. Tell me something new. Tell me your name."

"You must know that no slave has a name. No slave needs a name."

This time the lithe man reached out and did touch him, placing the palm of his hand over his heart with his fingers spread wide.

He felt the warmth inside him again even though his brain was telling him that the man's flesh was cold.

"I know," said the silver eyed man, "that the blood that flows through your veins yearns to feel the heat of a sun much hotter than the one that rises over these lands. And I know that you were not born to be a slave and that when you were named it was a name that was supposed to fill your people with hope and peace. So tell me your name."

It felt somehow disloyal, he wasn't sure whether to his Princess or to his previous life, to give his former name to this man, but either because he had become accustomed to obeying or the deeper, more hidden reason that he didn't want his conversation with this man to end, he answered the silver eyed creature's question.

"The name my father gave me was Grandre."

The other man wasn't laughing anymore, he looked serious. "Grandre, why do you want me? I've been part of your thoughts since you entered my domain."

"I don't understand what you mean. This is the first time we've met, so you cannot have been in my thoughts. And this is not your domain, this land is the domain of Princess Tatyanah and the royal family."

The man put a finger under Grandre's chin and raised his face so Grandre was looking at him, his silver eyes shone brighter then he let Grandre look away.

Grandre had been determined to continue staring at this man, but he couldn't; the pain in his head was greater than it had been before.

"You call me with your thoughts, but you don't know what I am," the other man said, "I am a wood nymph and you are searching for me."

"You are a wood nymph? But you look like a man."

The wood nymph brushed his finger down Grandre's cheek. "You know I am not an ordinary man." The wood nymph fanned his fingers out and gently caressed Grandre's neck, slowly moving down over Grandre's chest. "Your body knows I am not like any other man you have ever encountered."

"You are right that I have been ordered to find a wood nymph, and you are right that I do not know what one is, but if you truly are a wood nymph, then prove it to me," Grandre said, he called on his former warrior resolve and strength to keep his voice steady. His skin was shivering under the touch of this man, making his muscles feel weak as if his body's will was to fall to the ground at this man's feet.

The wood nymph's hand journeyed across his stomach, his fingers dipping into his belly button, and then the wood nymph's hand lost its gentleness and his fingers were firmly wrapped round the base of Grandre's hard manhood.

"I already have," the wood nymph said.

Grandre shook his head. He was finding it hard to focus his thoughts. It felt like the forest had somehow climbed into his mind. All he could taste and smell was the greenness of this world. He could hear the wind stirring the highest branches of the trees surrounding him.

"Tell me why you are searching for me, Grandre."

His real name on this creature's lips sounded like an enchantment. The wood nymph's fingers were moving, exploring his balls and caressing them; the wood nymph's other hand was on him now, finding the ridge on the underside of his hardness, his fingers encircling the head, spreading their heat through Grandre's sex.

"My Princess ordered me to capture you, a wood nymph, and bring you to her by moonrise."

"And what does your princess want to do with a wood nymph?" One of the wood nymph's hands was finding more of Grandre's body, pressing behind his balls, creeping up towards the centre of his buttocks.

"She wants to see me penetrated. She wants to see you penetrate me." Grandre's voice was gasps and moans. It felt like he was struggling to breathe, but when he did breathe he could taste all the fauna and flowers of the forest in the particles of air that rested on his tongue.

The tip of the wood nymph's finger slipped into the tight hole of Grandre's ass. His Princess had taken him more times than he could number, but the touch from this man made him feel like he was being parted for the first time.

"I don't care what she wants," the wood nymph said, there was disdain in his voice and he suddenly withdrew his touch from Grandre's body. Then his voice began softer, an aural caress, "What do you want, Grandre?"

Grandre couldn't answer. Without the wood nymph's touch on his skin he felt so cold, as if ice was in his veins.

"You do not need to answer," the wood nymph said placing a finger between Grandre's lips.

The heat blazed back through him, instinctively Grandre sucked on the wood nymph's finger, but the wood nymph pulled away again.

"I know what you want, Grandre." The wood nymph dropped to his knees and took Grandre's manhood in his mouth in one fluid movement.

Grandre could see every single fair hair that covered the nymph's body, he could see the nymph's eyes were not silver but they were the essence of all light, he could see the full redness of the nymph's lips encircling his sex. He could see all of his sex disappearing into the nymph's mouth. Then he couldn't see, all he could do was feel.

He had never experienced anything like the emotions racing through his body before. The wood nymph's hands were stroking his buttocks and all the pain in them from the Princess's beating had evaporated. He had no control over his own body, he couldn't contain his pleasure. His seed jetted deep into the nymph's throat. The wood nymph opened his mouth wide so Grandre could see his own juices in the other man's throat before the nymph swallowed hard and stood up to his full height, laughing.

"I know you now, Grandre. You gain more pleasure from one kiss from me than you have ever had from any woman, including your princess."

Grandre froze in shock.

"Go back to your princess and tell her I will visit her before moonrise."

Grandre didn't have a chance to reply—the nymph vanished. Grandre stood where he was, looking slowly around him. He could see nothing to prove that the nymph had ever been here. It could all have been his own dream. It had been a long time since the Princess had allowed him to sleep through the night, and she had been limiting his rations even though she worked him harder than any of her other pets. It could have all been his own hallucination. But he knew it had been real. He knew it with every nerve in his body. He knew it by the coldness that was now shrouding him like an ice cloak. As he thought so he realized that even if it was real and the wood nymph had been in front of him only moments previously, he couldn't with certainty know if he had indeed encountered a wood nymph, or if his initial thought that was a trick the Princess had set up to catch him betraying her was in fact correct.

He turned and began walking in the direction he believed would lead him back to Tatyanah.

She was pacing the room and had been since his return and his explanation. She had asked him so many questions and seemed to swiftly change between pleasure and fury at his answers. He had never known her so unsettled; she was like a different woman. The only thing he could be certain of was that the wood nymph had not been one of her servants. She had whipped him when she'd inspected his flesh and seen all the bruises and marks had disappeared, but then she had dropped to her knees and taken his manhood in her own mouth, something she had never done before, and when he released his seed she spat it on the floor and, looking disgusted, ordered him to lick his mess up.

She kept ordering him to the window to report on the progress of the day and the time until moonrise and was becoming increasingly agitated at his replies regarding the passing time.

"If I have done something wrong please inform me so I may correct my error," he said.

The Princess's pace increased and she did not look at him. "It is my fault, my fault," she said and then she did glance up at him and seemed to recall her position. "My fault for having faith in you," she said in her more usual proud tone. "Wood nymphs are dangerous. They are cunning creatures, they trick you, and they make weak minds like yours think you feel things that you can't possibly feel. It was stupid of me to believe you could handle one."

"Please forgive me, my Princess, for not being worthy enough to serve you," he said, "When the wood nymph arrives I will tell him to leave immediately."

"That wouldn't be very polite, Grandre," a familiar voice said, and Grandre turned away from his Princess to see the wood nymph was standing in his naked glory behind him. "Especially when I have been so looking forward to tasting your ass."

The Princess stepped between the two males with all her usual composure.

"You do not refer to my pet directly, you speak to me. I am the Princess Tatyanah of the family Jewelin, first daughter of the Queen of the Nine Courts." She gave the smallest bow permissible when making a first introduction.

"So I cannot speak to Grandre, but I can do this." He sidestepped around the Princess with a swiftness that she couldn't react to, placed his arms around Grandre's waist and embraced him, his tongue plunging deep into the other man's mouth.

It was only when the wood nymph had released his lips and was smiling challengingly at the Princess that Grandre considered how his Princess would want him to react. He was aware that he should have awaited her orders rather than responding to the wood nymph's touch but even now he couldn't pull away from him. He was too conscious of the other man's hardness pressing into the muscle of his stomach; he had a yearning to rub his own manhood against the wood nymph's.

"My pet found you under my orders; you are here to fuck him. Do it, and then leave."

The wood nymph lowered his hands so they were gripping Grandre's buttocks. "I don't take orders from you. Tell me why I should fuck this man just to satisfy your lust."

"To satisfy your lust too. You see the same thing in him that I do."

"No, girl, you are wrong. I see much more than you ever could." He kissed Grandre again, pressing his tongue deep into Grandre's mouth.

Grandre felt as if all his internal organs were aflame, but then the fire went out as the nymph released him and instead took Tatyanah in his arms and passionately kissed her. Tatyanah neither resisted or responded but when the wood nymph stepped away from her Grandre could see that her lips were slightly quivering and her hands were shaking and he knew she must be feeling the same as he was. For some reason this disappointed him.

"I don't care if you watch us," the wood nymph said to Tatyanah, "if it pleases Grandre." Then he turned to Grandre, his silver eyes shining like bright stars on a cloudy night. "I will not be gentle with you, as I know you do not like gentle. Get on your knees and spread your ass."

Grandre obeyed before Tatyanah had nodded her assent for him to obey the wood nymph's orders. He positioned himself as he had many times before for the princess, but this somehow felt different to anything he had known before. The princess entering him with a phallic object did not feel comparable to this wood nymph who would spread Grandre's flesh with his own flesh. He braced himself to feel pain, but the sensation when the wood nymph plunged his whole length into him was beyond pain. There was fire inside him, he felt like the whole heat of the sun was burning him up, sweat was dripping off his brow and down his back. He could not adjust to the feeling before the wood nymph pulled out and rammed into him again. The wood nymph's hand was on his back holding him down. He could not move. And the strange thing was that he didn't want to move, he wanted this fire to last forever. The pleasure it was giving him made him feel like he was being suffocated and transformed into a bird soaring through the skies at the same time.

The wood nymph seemed to be granting Grandre's silent wish and was pumping into his flesh with no end. Grandre's own body felt spent and was drained of all strength; every breath was a gasp, but the wood nymph was continuing to silently take him with the same energy as he had made his first thrust. Grandre turned his head to the side, wanting to find the mirror and gaze upon the vision of the other man's body entering his own, but instead he saw Tatyanah staring as if mesmerized at him. Her legs were spread, but her skirts still hung low, so he couldn't see what her hand was doing; however, he knew by the expression on her face she'd already experienced ecstasy several times. He wished for a moment he could be in her position, watching the wood nymph's slender body forcing into his own. He imagined the nymph's long fair hair rippling with the thrusts, the nymph's pale skin pushing against his own darker skin. It was an image of utmost beauty and perfection.

Then with a sudden shudder Grandre felt his body being filled with the seed of the wood nymph. The wood nymph gripped Grandre's hips firmly and seemed to somehow push himself deeper into him, as if he wanted to shoot his sperm into the centre of Grandre's very being. He held him there for a long time before finally he pulled away and Grandre was allowed to collapse onto the floor.

The room was silent, it felt like a peaceful caress and then the princess spoke. Even though he was in her bedchamber, Grandre had almost forgotten about her presence, or at least the way he was thinking about her was different to how he'd felt before he'd met the wood nymph.

"You can go now," she said.

Grandre thought for a moment she was addressing him, giving him his freedom, until the wood nymph's laughter tinkled through the room.

"I can go now," the wood nymph said and then laughed louder.

"I'm giving you permission. If you wish, I can call the guards and give you an order."

"You are so typical of your kind," the wood nymph said. "You do not belong here, Grandre. Let me take you home."

Grandre looked up to see that the wood nymph was holding his hand out to him.

"My pet belongs by my side. There is no other home for him."

"She has no power over me. I can take you home and no one in this land or any other will be able to stop me. You can be a man again. You can be Grandre, your name can be your people's hope instead of mourning."

Grandre looked at the nymph's hand reaching out, the long, elegant fingers. He thought about how 3warm their touch was, how cold this land suddenly felt to him.

"Creature, you are speaking out of place. He is my pet, you are wrong to tempt his stupid mind."

"Girl, you are wrong to deny anyone their freedom."

"She has not denied me my freedom, I chose to make a vow to her, and she has never forced me to do anything. She is my Princess." Grandre took a deep breath. "She is my Princess."

"Tell me you wish to stay with her and I will leave on my own."

Grandre could not look at him, could not even think about those silver eyes seeing into his most hidden thoughts.

"I wish to stay with her; every drop of blood in my body belongs to her."

"It is your choice," the wood nymph said. "You know how to find me, Grandre, when you want me."

The wood nymph vanished the same way he had done in the forest, no sign of magics, just gone.

The Princess came forward and gently stroked her pet's hair. "I really am very fond of you, little pet."

"Thank you," Grandre replied.

She pulled hard on a handful of his hair.

"Thank you for your grace, my Princess," he said.

"If you are good as you've proven yourself true to your vow I may let you play with your new little friend again."

"If it would not displease you, my Princess, I would rather not see the wood nymph again."

Tatyanah smiled. "I believe it would please me more to see you play with another of my pets; wood nymphs are far too disrespectful to join in our fun." Then her voice hardened. "And it was a bad influence on you; your behavior was not of the standard I expect from you. Fetch my whip."

He drew himself to his feet gave a low bow and walked across the room to obey her order. He shivered at the coldness he had never noticed before, with the knowledge that he would never feel warm again.

D- in Distress
Nadine Wilmot

Microwaved baked potatoes were terrible, but it was the cheapest thing on the menu, and Isibel was running out of cash. She picked at the withered thing with a desultory fork, trying to spread a little more evenly butter that, against all reason, refused to melt into the scalding spud-guts. She'd taken one glance at the prepackaged sour cream on offer—unrefrigerated since 1972, by the look of it—and passed on it. Her innards, she firmly believed, belonged inside.

The waitress oozed over to her table with a pot of road tar and topped off Isibel's mug. Her simpering smile flipped upside down when Isibel pushed the cup away and stood: while slim, her height was manly enough, but the lapels of her mangled leather coat slid enough to the side to reveal the admittedly minimal shape of her breasts, and the waitress' interest immediately evaporated. "Yer ticket," she sniffed, and with malice aforethought tore off the top sheet of paper from her scratch pad.

Isibel glanced at it and ripped someone else's order off the bottom; she handed both back to the affronted waitress, and dropped a fiver on the table to cover her actual bill. The tip was exorbitant for the service grudgingly offered, but she didn't feel like lurking long enough to get her change.

The night was a cold one. She stretched as the diner door swung to behind her, and took in a lungful of city air. It tasted of grease and smoke, and smelled worse. This close to the slums, she thought, it would. She was lucky she could breathe it without a mask. Bleeding lung was dreadfully common at city centers. She could deal with the smell. It could be so much worse.

She kicked a long leg over the seat of her motorcycle and gunned the engine to life. The bike purred its loud rumble between her legs, familiar as her own heartbeat. Isibel sat for a moment, half-leaning back to stare upward at a star-filled night sky no longer visible beyond the impenetrable orange glow of city lights. For a moment, she desperately missed the stars, a startling remembrance that brought a sharp heat to the corners of her eyes. Annoyed at herself, she shook her head, hooked her heel on the kickstand, tugged it up, and roared out of the parking lot onto the pothole-studded pavement.

The grubby motel that was temporarily home was only a mile or so away from the diner. It was a desperately cheap one, most of its rooms renting not by the night but by the hour. Isibel could afford better, but it was one of the very few in the area that allowed her kind to stay, so she took what she could get. Broken paving crunched like gravel under her wide tires as she turned into the parking lot. The paint on her door was peeling and chipped. It took three tries for the keycard to actually trigger the lock; she shoved open the door and closed it behind her with a click.

The room was simple—a bedroom, its heat and air conditioning unit jutting out from the wall beneath the window by the door; a small alcove in which was set a sink, a nonfunctioning coffeepot off to one side, a large, water stained mirror taking up the entire wall above it. The bathroom—a toilet and a shower—was off to the left, a doorless closet to the right.

Isibel dropped the keycard on the nightstand and flicked on the light over the sink. It took the fluorescent bulbs a moment or two to pop and flare, and when they did, the light they shed was pale and watery, and washed out her complexion to waxy corpse-white. She turned on the faucet and splashed tepid water over her face, then ran her hands through her short hair as she straightened. The face disinterestedly eyeing her back was a thin one, its habitual expression partly suspicious, partly disdainful, entirely closed off. Half-lidded dark eyes, dark hair, a narrow, downturned mouth, a pointed chin, a pointed nose—she looked sharp, in the most basic sense of the word. The kind of sharp that cut. For a moment she stared at herself, watching the inner flare of hatred reflected on her face, reflected in the mirror, then stomped the abrupt flash ruthlessly down. She tucked her hair, what strands of it would stay, behind ears that ended in delicately tapered, upswept points, and turned off the light once more; turned her back on the elf in the mirror.

She could still see in the gloom. It was a popular falsehood that the elvish could see in absolute darkness—even the best eyes required at least a little light—but her night vision was certainly superior to any human's. The edges of reddish streetlamp-glow that snuck past the closed curtain were enough to see by and anyway, it wasn't far to the bed.

There was a piece of paper on the nightstand. Isibel stopped, abruptly and tensely alert—she'd not put it there. But the only scent of anyone else in the room was the faint odor of the housekeeping staff which had obviously left hours before... It must have been left by them. Perhaps they were complaining about her towel usage. Clearly, one towel every third day was a strain on the motel's resources.

She sank to the edge of the bed and picked up the piece of paper, unfolded it carefully. Her brows rose in surprise: written in pidgin elvish, it was barely legible, but she was rather adept at deciphering the shorthand that her native tongue was becoming. It seemed the motel was far more egalitarian than most—while the more expensive hotels wouldn't admit her people existed, and the middle-brow chains wouldn't permit an elf to stay, whether or not they could afford the fee, this particular dive had apparently lowered itself so far as to employ one. The paper had, in fact, been left by the housekeeping staff. It was a badly copied flyer, the sort printed in off-brand copy shops with second- or thirdhand Xerox machines and insufficient supplies of toner. The handwriting on the original had been dreadful, and subsequent reproduction had not been kind to the text, but she picked through the slang and the shorthand, and smiled with all the warmth of old winter. A job. She'd take the following day to wrap up some errands, buy some provisions, find a man to sharpen her knives, and then, perhaps, she'd see what she could do to solve this little problem for someone. The flyer returned to the nightstand, and Isibel folded up on top of the coverlet and dropped into sleep.

The smell of the city did not improve by daylight, although that daylight was rapidly waning as she paused at a stoplight. She'd finished her checklist of errands; she'd restocked her supplies. The bike was tuned; her saddlebags were refilled; she'd checked out of the seedy motel. Now... the job. She half-closed her eyes for a moment. The city's streets flashed rapid-fire past her mind's eye, tracing her route to the address on the flyer; *there* it was. The point was a beacon now, tugging at her unerringly as a bird's migration. The light changed, flaring green; she shot forward before the SUV behind her could get any ideas about right-of-way, and headed in the direction of the incessant pull.

The smell worsened as she followed the road deeper into the inner-city ghettos. It thickened into something she could taste, tinny at the back of her throat, and also familiar—the old industrial centers, abandoned by humans, were habitually inhabited now by elves. It was a homecoming every time she rode into the slums of any city, anywhere. There was another component to the smell here, though, something with a heavier smoke than the old factories could rightly account for. The taste of ash accumulated with the smells of defunct industrialism and poverty, and when she finally halted, tires screaming, in the empty space that served as a de facto town square, her scowl had carved deep lines into her narrow face.

Burning rubber now mixed with the other scents, but that was a comfort. Isibel dropped her kickstand and stood, long legs straddling the motorcycle while several slender figures emerged from doorways surrounding the open area. She tugged the flyer out of her pocket and waved it contemptuously at each of them, ashamed of her anger even as it flamed, misdirected. It wasn't their fault they lived like this, not really. Not when the deck was so obviously and thoroughly stacked against them. Against her.

"I'm here," Isibel said loudly, "about the dragon."

The word—spoken in her native elvish—silenced the murmurings of the gathering crowd. They stared at her. She stared back. Only one of them held her eyes, stepping forward to touch two fingers to her shoulder in ritual respect. "Bless you for offering," the elderly elf said sorrowfully, "but you'll die if you try this alone. Don't you have... friends?"

Isibel held out the flyer to him; he took it automatically; then, as though unsure what else to do with his hands, held onto it like a talisman.

"I'm not good at friends," she told him, and swung her leg over the motorcycle, leaving it propped on its kickstand. His eyes roamed over her and the bike, taking in the small arsenal secured behind the seat, across the saddlebags. His mouth turned up in a sardonic little half-smile as he came to the only conclusion possible, and he nodded.

"That," he answered, "should perhaps have been obvious. I can't offer pay," he continued. Hearing the best reason for not taking a job, Isibel cocked a brow. "But anything recovered from its hoard is yours. It's only stolen our families from us, but it goes out foraging in the rest of the city. All that glitters." The old elf's tone matched the ashy air for bitterness.

Dragons were cruel creatures, Isibel knew. They enjoyed playing games with people in the same manner that cats enjoyed playing with battered mice, and they were known for playing long games, and subtle ones. Suffering was, to them, spice; fear the most delectable flavor.

Secretly, Isibel understood that pleasure, and was ashamed. However many elves the beast had stolen from this shanty-town, none of them would have had an easy death, or a quick one.

Isibel looked around herself at the silent gathering—the entire population of the shantytown seemed to have assembled by now—and came to a decision. Far be it from her to take the part of paladin—mercenaries made more profit—but there were more kinds of payment than money.

If nothing else, it never hurt to pad her reputation.

"I'll deal with it," she said.

Isibel hauled a small backpack out of one of the saddlebags as the crowd slunk away, returning to their corners and lofts and crowded rooms. It took her a minute to chain the bike securely to the nonfunctional lamppost that served as the central fixture of the square, but once secured, it was safe enough. The enchantment woven through her chain and padlocks had cost her a staggering amount of money, but it was a good spell. Nothing she owned would wander away, that was certain. A few hours' sleep would rest her well enough, and tomorrow... tomorrow, she would take a look around. Sniff about. *Plan*.

A younger elf, lean and slightly taller than she, approached her as she straightened. Gently touching her shoulder with two fingertips, he bowed his head. "My mother and I," he murmured in their native elvish, "would be honored if you will stay with us. There's no motel," he continued, confirming the obvious. In fact, there had been a derelict Motel 6 about a mile outside the slum, its parking lot cracked and overgrown with the hardy, ugly weeds that were the only plants that would grow in the area. "But there is an extra bed in our home. My father is gone."

Gone could mean so many things. Dead? Taken in one of the periodic "employment drives" that humans were so keen on, drafting desperate elves as cheap labor for jobs deemed unsuitable for human hands to perform? Or just... gone, disappeared one day to seek the potential for better fortune in another city where, perhaps, prejudices were not quite so stark and unshakeable. Isibel could have told him he was wasting his time. She'd been in many cities, and they were identical in their loathing for her people.

Or perhaps he had been taken by the dragon. Isibel would not ask so rude a question. He was simply... gone, and those left in his absence would silently, privately mourn, and that would be an end of it.

The bed was a traditional hammock, a curve of cloth strung in an alcove at the back of the tiny house. Isibel thanked her host— Adryn, his name was—and his mother when they brought a much-mended blanket for her. She pulled off her boots and settled without undressing further into the gentle parabola of canvas. The hammock was angled such that she could see a generous slice of the house's common area and she watched, privately pleased, while Adryn enfolded the petite form of his mother in a close embrace. He kissed the elderly elf-maid's forehead, smiled down at her, and quietly bid her goodnight. Isibel approved. Respect and love for one's elders was... unfashionable, now: another human trend desperately mimicked by elven youth in a futile bid for acceptance by the majority. It took very little time for her to drop entirely into dreamless sleep.

She'd been out picking through the inner-city detritus of abandoned buildings and forgotten streets for several hours the next morning when the cry went up. Isibel was not terribly far away from the tenement, and legged it back at a sprint. The elderly male elf met her at the entrance to the square, hugging himself tightly; behind him, a matronly sort, uncut hair hanging stringy in her face, sobbed on her knees inside a circle of comforters.

"Her son," the elder said, a hitch in his voice. "Her son was taken—it took him, dragged him off the street. It was too fast for anyone to follow."

Isibel eyed him narrowly, then caught a glimpse of the woman's face when she dragged her rough sleeve over her eyes. The hunter's heart sank: Adryn's mother. Isibel nodded. "Her son," she confirmed. "And your...?"

"Nephew," he said, and looked away. Behind him, the woman collapsed forward, hair mingling with the dust of broken pavement, her weeping gone silent, for all that it shook her like a terrier with a rat.

Isibel looked from one to the other, then rolled her shoulders back, popping vertebrae in her neck. She strode past the grieving elves and unfastened the padlocks on her motorcycle to get access to her gear. After a moment's contemplation, she took from her saddlebags only two knives. Guns were laughably useless against the dragonfolk, but a good steel blade was still as keen a dragonbane as it had ever been.

"I'll bring him back," Isibel growled, and turning away from them, headed out of the tenements.

It took her much of the rest of the day to locate what, she was reasonably certain, was the entrance to the beast's den. The haze-layered sun was well into its descent when she arrowed in on an old office building that had collapsed inward upon itself. There was a path scraped through the rubble, and amongst the footprints of scavenging elves and stray animals were hints of what could only be described as... slithering: whipcoil lengths of smoothed ground with, here and there, a mark that was easy to imagine had been made by supernaturally-hard scale scraping against stone. Isibel stood before the entrance, hands on her hips, and flared her nostrils. Yes. This was it. Here, the acrid smoke-smell was stronger, emanating like invisible poison from amongst the piles of cracked and crumbling masonry.

Where the door had been now leaned a post-and-lintel entryway of concrete, a modern recreation of the old circles from an older country. Mouth thinned in a determined line, Isibel strode forward and, a knife in either hand, passed through from gritty, red city-light into the darkness beyond.

It took a moment for her eyes to adjust to the gloom. There was a pathway through the destruction here, just as there had been outside. It led deeper into the remnants of the destroyed building, swerving around large chunks of masonry and past pitted, cracked support beams, some still miraculously upright, holding up a roof that was no longer there. It led back, and downward. The floor had collapsed when the building had, and the pathway descended steeply. There had been a basement, now little more than a rubble-filled pit, and where the basement wall had been now gaped another hole, broken through the cement blocks into the disused sewer beyond.

The smell was much stronger here. Isibel sidestepped through the rough-edged hole, breathing shallowly through her mouth; the scent was nearly a physical burn in her nostrils. Old sewage was a pungent undertone to the higher, sharper smell of ash and smoke, and the odorous cocktail clogged her nose with an overload of sensory input, making it impossible to separate threads of scent from each other and follow just one. All she could do was ignore it all and rely on other senses.

It was easy enough to find a trail, of sorts. The same scales that had scraped odd markings into the broken concrete outside had burnished the walkway lining the sewer. Isibel followed this, pacing herself. There was no telling how far into the city's underbelly the beast had made its lair. There were occasional tributaries where the dragon had now and then taken side-passageways, but the majority of its travels, it seemed, had been made with unbroken single-mindedness of purpose: straight out, and straight back in.

The smell gradually grew into something she could almost taste as she wound her way further along the labyrinthine tunnels. At least, Isibel mused absently, the sewers were not used as sewers anymore, not this deep into the city's guts. Plumbing was a luxury her people couldn't afford. Like the mountain folk of the early twentieth century, the elves used outhouses and counted themselves lucky to have the wood to build them.

Smoke stung her eyes and the back of her throat as she walked; the temperature was rising. She paused a moment to wipe sweat off her brow and froze. Her elongated ears twitched slightly as she strained to listen, uncertain—no, she had not been mistaken.

Movement. There was an arch a couple of yards behind her, and Isibel darted back, ducked into it, and flattened herself against the brick wall, stilling her breath and slowing her heartbeat. She couldn't sustain that stillness for long, but a minute or so would be all she needed, long enough to go unsuspected. A dragon couldn't smell anything, its olfactory sense burned away early in its life by its own stench: like her, here, it would have to rely on vision and hearing, and if she didn't move, didn't make a sound...

The sound of movement resolved now into something readily discernible, and Isibel frowned. Those were footfalls. She moved out of the archway in time to hook an arm around the throat of a slender form as it stumbled past, and lowered her knife almost as soon as she'd raised it.

"Adryn," she murmured against the elf's neck and his legs collapsed from beneath him. Half-sobbing, half-gasping for breath, he sank to his knees, his entire body trembling.

"It's you," he choked out. "It's—I thought it had got me again, I thought—it left, and it hasn't come back yet and I managed to find my way this far—"

Isibel sheathed her blades and hauled him to his feet.

"If it's gone, it will be coming back and gods only know how long we've got. Let's go."

She supported much of his weight as they ran, guiding him along the scraped-stone pathway she'd used to wend her way in from the outside. Adryn didn't speak further, but allowed her to lead him at a pace he clearly would not be able to sustain for long. She hoped he wouldn't have to. Her heart was pounding, more from anticipatory dread than physical strain, when they finally reached the hole in the basement that led out of the sewers and into the destroyed office building. There was no sign of the dragon as they hurried up the rubble-strewn pathway and out onto the abandoned, overgrown street.

Night had well and truly fallen by now. Isibel had no idea what time it was, but there was little illumination but the ambient amber-yellow glow of city-lights from the more prosperous human areas. The reddish glow filtered through smog and dirty air to cast enough light to see by with elven eyes, even if it was with difficulty. Isibel led Adryn back through the ghost town of abandoned industrial complexes and long-disused strip malls until the warm yellow lights of elven lanterns finally came into view.

There was nobody waiting for them in the square. Nobody expected either of them to return, Isibel knew, and she was just as glad they were unheralded. What she wanted most in the world right now was the hammock that was her temporary bed, and sleep.

Adryn's mother was awake, however. She rose to her feet when they entered, and cried out in shocked delight.

"Adryn! Gods and Watchers be praised, you're alive!" She

threw her arms around him, sobbing her joy. The young elf, blushing in embarrassment, turned out of her embrace and then, as an afterthought, leaned down to kiss her cheek. "I'm tired," he told her. "It was—it was unspeakable. I want to sleep."

His mother patted his cheek. "Off you go," she said, and smiled indulgently. As he left them to climb the ladder to the upper floor where he slept, his mother turned to Isibel. "You have done the impossible," she whispered. "You brought my boy home to me, and I thought he was lost forever."

Isibel cupped the elderly elf's shoulder with one hand, and smiled thinly, watching Adryn disappear into the loft. "There's still the dragon to deal with," is all she said, and prowled past the elderly woman to collapse into her own hammock.

Adryn came to her much later that night, after his mother had finally exhausted her joyful tears and taken herself off to bed. Isibel, who had not yet fallen asleep, watched the shape of his body as he stepped silently into the alcove and paused beside her.

"Forgive me intruding," he whispered in her ear, "but... I wished to thank you for my rescue. I would have, I'm sure, remained lost in that maze if you hadn't come. I'd be dead by now. The dragon—" He stopped, the word breaking as he spoke it, and finally shook his head and continued. "Anyway. I wanted to thank you." His fingertips glided down her cheek, along the firm line of her narrow jaw. "Personally."

Isibel sat up and swung her legs over the side of the hammock; it swayed gently. He was handsome enough, she decided, eyeing the planes of his face partially illuminated by the dim light of the single lantern left lit in the main room. A bit thin, even for an elf, but so was she; so were they all. He had a strong jaw, and pale green eyes that caught the light like muted gems as he watched her stand.

There were, indeed, more kinds of payment than money, and more ways than one to find pleasure in a killing job.

She took his hand and lifted it to her lips, kissed his palm and each of his fingertips. He sighed, and she let her mouth drift to his wrist, briefly, sharply biting there, and kissing away the sting when he gasped. A few steps forward and she'd pinned him against the wall and claimed his mouth in a relentless kiss; she stole his breath as he inhaled and breathed it back into him; tasted the line of his teeth and the almost delicate shape of his lips with the tip of her tongue. He groaned and Isibel pressed her hips against his, softly growling her pleasure when she felt his arousal already rigid and ready, constrained by his torn jeans. Her hands fell to the hem of his faded t-shirt, and she tugged it upwards, forcing him to lift his arms so she could take it off him.

She did not. Instead twisting the fabric around his wrists, she pinned them above his head. With a wolfish grin, she bit her way down the slender length of his neck, delighting in the tiny movements he made. She kissed along his collarbone and down; took a nipple in her mouth and suckled there for a moment; bit it, then withdrew an inch or two to gently blow a teasing stream of cool air across its erect surface. Adryn squirmed, biting back a soft cry.

Taking pity, Isibel released his hands; they fell to her shirt and tugged at it, finally finding the zipper that held it closed. He drew it down; the fabric parted and fell away to reveal her bare chest, breasts small enough not to require support. His thumbs smoothed over her nipples, fingers fanning over the petite curve of her breasts; he traced the narrow girth of her ribcage with his palms and finally found the fastenings of her fitted, matte-leather pants.

Isibel pulled down the zipper of his jeans as he pushed the leather trousers over the swell of her rear; she stepped back and out of them, and jerked him forward, away from the wall. One shove of her hand sent him back and down; he caught himself and sprawled on the floor. She was on him in a moment's time, savagely pulling his jeans down and off his legs, leaving him nude beneath her.

She straddled him, pinning his shoulders against the floor, and bent to kiss him again, fiercely, declaring her ownership. He made eager, desperate noises against her mouth, hands cupping her bared buttocks and sliding up over her hips, over the muscled plane of her back, around to the diminutive mounds of her breasts. His cock rode hard against the inside of her thigh, shifting as they moved, teasing her with its presence; she reached between them to cradle it, tracing its length and girth with curious fingers.

"Beautiful," she whispered, and licked his neck with a salacious tongue. "Perfect."

"You absolutely are," he replied in a rough whisper. "I knew when I saw you—I had to have you. What a prize you are..."

Isibel rose up on her knees, straightening above him. He stared up at her, green eyes glazed with want.

"Put your hands above your head," she murmured to him through a crooked smile. "Let me look at you. Let me take you like that."

Adryn obeyed, curling his hands around the hammock-post. Isibel gazed at him possessively, then reached between his legs to stroke his erection; his eyes closed and he delicately arched his back, and as he did so, she lowered her body to engulf his cock completely.

He filled her; she wasn't surprised. It had been some time since she'd taken a lover, and he was of a good size. When Isibel growled at his girth inside her, it matched a low moan from him. She leaned forward and rolled her hips back and down, reveling in the roiling heat that began to swell within her, the beginnings of pleasure. It wouldn't take long, she knew. Not tonight. Adryn rolled his hips upward to match her movements, and she rocked with him, the edges of her self-control fraying as his thrusts, too, gradually grew rougher, edged with desperation. When finally the heat in her belly boiled to fever-pitch, it brought crashing around her a silent, stark implosion of shuddering ecstasy, a tight throbbing that clenched her sex around his cock like a heartbeat. The heat of his own orgasm exploded inside her. She collapsed on top of him, both of them panting, and she let her hand skitter seemingly of its own volition into the pile of her belongings beneath the hammock.

Adryn had started to laugh delightedly when her knife slid abruptly between his ribs, upward into his heart. The laugh choked, became a gurgling scream that swelled into a bestial roar. Isibel threw herself off the writhing body on the floor, jerking her knife out as she went. One stab was all it took: it had been a true one.

Adryn's mother came running, screaming, toward the little alcove; Isibel twisted to her feet and tackled the elderly elf-woman, bearing her to the floor. A heavy coil of scaled, many-jointed tail whipped over their heads and slammed down against the floor, narrowly missing them both. Isibel rolled to the side, then dragged the other woman to the far side of the room while the thrashing thing that had borne Adryn's form flailed with decreasing strength and then, finally, stopped.

"How did you know?" the elderly elf whispered, staring at the dragon's corpse. It was malformed, caught by death in the process of transforming from the shape it had stolen back into its own; a long tail uncoiled from the hunched torso of a slim elf, its spine a series of bony ridges halted in the process of bursting skin. Black blood pooled thick and malodorous beneath the body, slowly oozing from the wound she had inflicted.

Isibel tore her gaze away from the twisted corpse, and smiled sadly at Adryn's mother.

"He pushed you away," she said, and shrugged. "I knew then. He pushed you away when he should have held you tightly enough to crush you."

"But—but you—I knew he would come to you but if you knew already, how could you—"

Isibel didn't answer. She prowled past the beast's corpse to retrieve her clothing and the sheath for her knife where it had lain beneath her hammock. When she had dressed, she guided the sobbing mother out of the house, and wordlessly handed her into the care of her brother.

It was safe enough to go back to the dragon's hole the next day. Isibel went with three others, leading them to the destroyed office, through its accumulated rubble and down into the disused bowels of the city. They whispered amongst themselves as she prowled along the scale-smoothed path, following it deeper today than she had managed the day before, threading her way along the dragon-road to the heart of it.

There was, indeed, all that glittered to be found at the center of the labyrinth. No legendary stockpile of glittering coins and chalices, still the arched convergence of several tunnels contained a treasure trove of expensive electronics, bundled cash, and a variety of other items that had caught the dragon's wandering attention during its predations. Isibel took a significant portion of the cash and several guns from the carefully-piled hoard, as well as a handful of ostentatious gold chains and charms. The dragon had apparently raided a pawnshop at some point in its career; well, she'd return all these things to pawn and take her pay in more cash.

They found Adryn toward the back of the hoard. Isibel was surprised—she'd honestly thought him dead, when the beast had inadvertently broken its cover the previous night. That he was not startled her. The elves who had accompanied her gently lifted his unconscious form and, taking turns carrying him, headed back the way they had come. She followed at a slower pace. When finally Isibel reached the tenements, she all but ignored the calls and ragged cheers of the slum's denizens, waving off those who approached. She loaded her salvage from the hoard into her saddlebags, and stuffed her chain and padlocks in after them. Swinging a leg over the seat, she straddled the motorcycle and fired the engine into roaring life. There were other cities and other jobs and, probably, other dragons. When Isibel peeled out of the square onto the road, it didn't occur to her to look back.

Primè Nocta
Kierstin Cherry

Lightning fractured the night sky and in the burning afterglows, the Apothecary loomed before her. Rain sheeted down upon its hulking mass, and mist rose from the summer stones that ringed its gloomy entrance.

Alone, Zana stood at the crossroads—a ghost in the hazy night. Soaked to the skin, she gathered her wedding gown about her and ran.

She passed into the shadow of the building, her feet splashing through small pools upon the broken flagstones. She hugged the rusted iron fence, brushing past soaked hemlocks and nightshade. Already, the color was bleeding out of the night. The rain on her flushed skin felt like nothing more than water falling.

She was dying.

Slipping through the gate, Zana stopped before the Apothecary's darkened maw. Reflexively, she clenched her hands into fists. Across her knuckles, emerald-green scales cracked, painfully desiccated and withering.

"Magden." She whispered the name of her queen, but it was lost in the clamor of the storm. Magden would know what to do.

A deathly chill gripped her as she ran up the broken steps. The scent of antiquity and old medicine eddied a vaporous pall around the Apothecary, the musk of a serpent's den lingering a warning about its shadow-thrown entrance. Heedless, Zana plunged over the threshold.

Darkness enshrouded her, pierced only by the guttering of crimson candles in the chamber beyond. Shadows distended, forms once familiar now lost to the darkness. She strained to penetrate the veil, but her night vision was steadily failing. Fear threaded its way through her dying frame. Heart spasming, she trembled back.

Deep in the darkness, the echoing hiss of a snake's brood awakening.

Panic burst open in her breast. Zana ran, fleeing toward the flickering candles, blinded by light and darkness, cobwebs catching across her face and in her hair. Sobs wracked her through, augmenting her agony—her body dying all around her. The hem of her wedding gown snagged a splintered board. Weeping, she tore it free and stumbled.

The small of her back connected with an oaken table. A hitching breath caught the reek of old blood, sending a flash of animal fright through her. Whirling, she backed up, candlelight mocking in her eyes.

A dozen scarlet pillars had been set to burn upon a huge oak table, their light guttering over a butchery of bloodstains, a surgeon's array of incisions gashed across slowly-rotting wood.

Lightning lashed the night. A nest of asps hissed in the falling darkness.

Breath stolen, Zana froze. Droplets of rain fell from her hair and trickled down into her cleavage. Wedding silk clung to flushed skin. She tried not to recall the look of betrayal on her betrothed's face.

He had not understood.

Across her entire body, emerald serpent-scales molted, peeling back to reveal human flesh beneath. Her limbs had lost their reptilian strength, their sinuous flexibility. Her fangs had fallen out hours ago. How long before the final death of her Nythian blood? How long before she became fully human?

She remembered that night—the storm, the ritual—she remembered...

"Magden?"

The kiss of her queen's blade through her half-blood flesh. Zana's gaze fell once more to the oaken slab. Blood and crimson wax spilling. That night—

"Magden!" *That night you killed me upon this altar!*

"Zana."

Her breath crystallized.

Of course, Magden had been there all along, ensconced in shadow and gloom. She was queen, the Primè Reinè of the Nyth, and she could sense the presence of all her people, even a dying half-blood.

Heart tripping on fear and death, Zana searched the shadows, seeking to divide Magden's willowy figure from the darkness. Her human eyes were painfully inadequate.

A low chuckle carried on the hissing of serpents, and the Reinè revealed herself. A gown of vesperis silk clung, shimmering blue-back upon her sinuous body. The candlelight caught her red hair like a fiery halo and burned a serpentine glow in her grey eyes.

The sight of her pierced Zana's heart. The memory of another night arose—lying in Magden's arms, the night they nearly followed the example of their mothers, Nyth queen and Zephyris concubine.

Thunder boomed through the Apothecary, and a flash of lightning burned the image of Magden's face into her—a porcelain visage bejeweled with fine cobalt scales, her eyes the color of a storm, black pupils slitted and pulsing with reptilian desire.

Guilt blushing upon her face, Zana allowed her gaze to wander the vivid strokes of scale ornamenting the Reinè's body, trailing down both sides of her neck and along her collarbones, plunging down her cleavage to form a V between her breasts. The vesperis gown obscured further exploration, but Zana's thoughts delved deeper to the soft snakeskin that defined Magden's ribs and her hipbones, joining between her legs to cover her feminine sex.

A pleasured hiss drew Zana's attention. The Reinè had caught her looking.

With slow, delicious dread, Zana realized that she had groped down over her own bosom to her thighs where her hands clenched the sodden wedding gown in frustration. The wet silk clung tight to her body, making it easy for the Reinè to appraise every inch of her. Meeting her gaze, Magden smiled, sharp in the candlelight.

Buried deep within Zana's dying blood, a visceral twinge leapt and twisted. Had her mother felt the same euphoria when Queen Margrethe had looked upon her?

But her hands, her scales, the death that gripped her! Zana crumpled before her Reinè. "Magden, what's happening to me?"

"It's what you wanted, isn't it?" Magden's voice was sultry. "When you came to me that night, you forsook your Nythian blood. You begged me that you might re-awaken fully human."

A musky scent wafted from her scales, alluring even to Zana's dulling senses, lighting her body with a sudden ache. "What did you do to me?"

"You wanted to be free. To marry the man you love."

The perfume of her serpent-flesh was intoxicating, awakening the part of Zana that was still Nyth, still Zephyris concubine. "I—" She had forgotten how compelling Magden was, how enthralling to be a Nyth in the presence of the queen. Magden's snakeskin scent was strong, overpowering the odor of dust and old remedies, overpowering even the ozone of the storm.

They were fated to be the perfect match—the Primè Reinè of the Nyth and her Zephyris—genetically encoded, destined to breed, every cell, every fragment of them predisposed to the act of mating.

Fear electrified Zana's spine. She knew the truth of Magden. Primè Reinè, Nyth Queen—voracious, hermaphroditic, driven by instinct. To lie with her was to bear her young.

"You still wish to forsake me?" Magden's eyes glowed in the gloom.

Sudden desire strangled Zana, the last vestiges of her Nythian blood fighting its inevitable demise. The ache inside became a blossoming burn. "Yes."

Magden lingered, close but just out of reach. "You wish to wed this man?"

The Reinè's fragrance beguiled Zana, perfuming her skin, making her heady. Zana took the last half-step and their bodies gently collided. "Yes..."

With a jolt, Zana felt it—the genetic reaction that shivered through Magden's tall frame, their proximity awakening the insatiable instinct to breed. Chemical response became need, and need blossomed into full, unfettered lust. Magden reached out, her hands falling possessively to Zana's hips. Zana, too, felt the weight of her genetics, her body burning with desire, uncontrolled and writhing against Magden, her mind reeling with the urge to arouse her further.

For a moment, they lost themselves in the embrace, Reinè and Zephyris, entwined around each other in the first throes of their mating passion.

Magden's grip tightened, pulling Zana close, hips to hips, slowly grinding. The half-blood girl moaned, her hands tangling in Magden's red hair.

Thunder crashed discordant, and the spattering of lighting cut sharp through the night.

"If you wish to wed him, then why are you not in his bed?"

Zana's desire withered like her dying scales.

Magden began to pull away. She was mastering herself. "You are no longer one of mine."

Zana couldn't bear her absence. She reached out. "Magden..."

"You have chosen affinity with your human half." The Reinè took Zana's hands from her face. She stepped back. "Even now, your Nythian blood dies within you. Soon, you will no longer be my Zephyris."

Bereft, distraught, Zana put a hand to her head. Vertigo gripped her skull.

"I will no longer be your Reinè."

Zana reeled. That was what she wanted, wasn't it? Her throat closed painfully.

Before her, Magden stood, wonderful and terrible, gentle and yet dire and frightening. Zana trembled in her presence. Her Nythian blood would not be quieted. "No...Magden, I—" With a stifled sob, she threw herself into the arms of her queen.

Over her cries, Zana could hear the storm's song fading fast in her ears. Only the Nyth could hear the mesmeric dirge of rain and thunder. All around her, storm and lightning, her world was coming down. She buried her face in Magden's shoulder, breathing deep of her enthralling scent. One hand tangled into Magden's red curls as if she would never let go.

The Primè Reinè resisted, but Zana urged against her, relentless, inflaming her primitive urges. Reptilian muscles rippled. Moisture beaded on cobalt-blue scales. Magden's body shuddered, trapped in a chrysalis of desire.

Drawn by the sultry lure of serpent-flesh, Zana leaned in, tonguing the dewdrops of natura that glistened on Magden's scales. The snaky softness rippled under her kisses, the taste slightly metallic, the scent overpowering.

Remaining still, the Reinè suffered her Zephyris's caress. Her eyes glowed a serpentine sheen in the candles' light, a pleasured hiss she could not master growling deep in her throat. Her body trembled with need, instinctual, inevitable, but she did not make a move to claim her concubine. One fang caught her lower lip, drawing a bead of green blood.

Eagerly, Zana pressed her open mouth to it, sampling the slow burn of Magden's agony. She brought her hands to her Reinè's face and held it. "Why do you hesitate?"

"As the Goddess of Storms and Secrets is my witness, I abandoned my claim upon you." Magden's voice was a whisper. "I gave you freely."

Zana closed her eyes. "I know." She was stricken under the weight of what she might do.

"Once we begin, neither one of us will be in control." Magden trembled, her body already gripped in the initial throes. "It is the way of the Primè Reinè and her Zephyris. We will lose ourselves to the act."

"The act?"

"Of mating."

Zana could not suppress a shiver of anticipation.

Magden's grey eyes dilated black. "If we mate, then human or Nyth, you will bear my brood."

The shuddering thought of Magden impregnating her—Zana's human sensibility recoiled in fear and revulsion. But her Nythian half strained closer, sudden lust dispersing fear like smoke.

Running her hands up her body, she cupped her small breasts, pushing them against Magden's, massaging the Reinè's bosom with her own. The wet silk of her wedding gown shifted, threatening to expose the entirety of her cleavage.

Magden remained still though her eyes burned with lust.

Moaning, Zana rubbed herself harder, straining for Magden's touch. The slick feel of snakeskin against her hot, dying flesh was more than she could bear. Frustrated, she grabbed Magden's hands and pressed them to her breasts. A low groan escaped her as she began to massage herself. Pleasure slivered up her spine, staving off the fright, the pain of a part of herself expiring.

A shaky breath quivered from Magden's lips. Zana entwined their fingers, guiding, groping. Urging closer, she yearned to the tips of her toes and pulled her Reinè down to meet her. Her lips found the softness of Magden's, and she kissed, opening her mouth. Her tongue licked cautiously, sampling the sharpness of serpent fangs.

Her wedding gown crumpled under the force of Magden's grip.

A smile rose to Zana's lips. Her queen could not fight genetics forever. A willing Zephyris, she writhed, rolling her hips to meet Magden's.

With serpentine speed, Magden shoved her hard against the oak table. The candles rocked and one tipped over, running red across the butchered surface. Zana shivered as her Reinè pinned her. She arched back, leaning against the oak. The Reinè's body came against hers and this time, there was no hesitation.

Slow and hard, Magden rode her against the altar. Her leg slipped between Zana's, her hips shoving the Zephyris back against the table.

Zana moaned and fought forward, sliding her sex against Magden's thigh. The pressure on her clit was pure, liquid torment, the silk of her panties growing damp.

Magden bent her head. Her red curls fell forward, caressing Zana's face. Grey eyes saturnine, she crushed her closer, returning the kiss, opening her mouth, tonguing deep to taste her Zephyris.

Thunder boomed, and Zana broke away, gasping from the intensity. The silk of her wedding gown was wet and not from the rain. Without ceremony, she hiked it up and sank back down, straddling her Reinè's leg.

The touch of Zana's hot thighs against hers caught Magden breathless. She rested her forehead against her Zephyris's collarbone, her lips hovering over barren and peeling scales. "My dying Zana." Softly, she licked. The green scales glistened emerald-wet with her saliva, taking on an almost healthy luster.

Moaning, Zana rode her, silk panties and vesperis gown growing damp under her lusty ministrations. Her fingernails dug into Magden's shoulders, igniting tension within serpentine skin.

It was not enough.

Desperate, she sank to her knees before her Reinè. She did not know what she meant to do. Magden leaned back, placing both hands on her altar.

Softly, Zana pressed her lips to her Reinè's feet. Her hands came up to caress Magden's calves, slipping under vesperis silk. She reveled in the feel of Magden's bare flesh—of the soft scales that adorned her shins and knees and trailed a soft pattern to her inner thighs.

The gown was tight, clinging to Magden's skin with a mixture of sweat and the natura from her scales. Eagerly, Zana tore it, splitting the fabric all the way to the Reinè's sex.

Magden cried out and dug her fingernails into the oak. Looking down, she met the gaze of her Zephyris. Zana's green eyes burned bright with lust. Magden could not control herself—it was the way of the Primè Reinè and her chosen concubine. She lifted her torn skirts and straddled Zana's face. "Open your mouth."

Her Zephyris instincts pulsing within her, Zana opened her mouth to receive her Reinè. The sultry heat of scales and their soft touch upon her lips dizzied her. She flicked her tongue, licking satiny smooth and hot. Light perspiration mingled with the Reinè's natura, forming a heady sheen that she lapped covetously.

She pressed her face between Magden's legs, parting her wider, exploring, seeking to find the seam that hid her innermost flesh. Her breath came hard against supple scales, inhaling the musky taste of her Reinè.

Moaning, Magden clenched her hands in Zana's short hair and shifted against her mouth. Scales split, and her natura ran sticky-hot over her Zephyris's face. Baptized, Zana opened her mouth wide, drinking the deluge of her Reinè's sluttish juices. It sluiced down her throat, pushing its way into her, burning her with the lust of queen and concubine.

Gasping, she probed with her tongue, working her way deeper, splitting the cleft further. Her hands gripped her Reinè's inner thighs, fingernails biting into soft flesh. In long, licking strokes, Zana took her, slipping her tongue over hot, swollen lips and into Magden's shuddering hole.

With an almost human gasp, the Primè Reinè lurched forward, red curls falling into her face. In the candlelight, her eyes glowed lustful, sinister. Her slitted pupils dilated wide, and she gave a fanged smile down at her Zephyris. Her eyes rolled back and she groaned, her hips writhing. She let her chemical instincts take her.

Something nudged against Zana's mouth. A hard shaft pushed its way between her lips and down her throat. Slick and soft yet rigid, it pulsed inside her like a living member.

Zana nearly choked with the effort of accommodating it all. She pulled back and the shaft slipped from her mouth. Instinctively, her hand came up to caress it. Long and thick, silken-smooth and covered with cobalt scales hard as lapis, it was as real as any man's.

Magden swayed slightly in anticipation.

Meeting her glowing gaze, Zana began to caress her. The skin leaped and twitched at her touch. She bent her head to kiss, and then took the phallus in her mouth, full and firm. As soon as her lips closed around the tip, Magden pushed, sliding it down her throat.

Zana relaxed. Her Reinè's fingers brushed the hair from her forehead. Slowly, Magden began to thrust. Her breath came short and quick, her strokes long and precise, driving down deep into her Zephyris's throat.

Struggling for breath, Zana pursed her lips, licking as Magden withdrew and sucking as she pumped. One hand grabbed her Reinè's hip for purchase while the other gripped the root of Magden's cock, stroking the supple hardness before venturing further. Just behind, she found the feminine sex wet and waiting. Her fingers fluttered against the outer scales, then probed deeper, spreading Magden's soaked pussy, sampling the torrid juices. The twin scents of female sex and male musk anointed her blushing face.

Shuddering, Magden watched, her eyes dilating as her hard shaft slipped between her concubine's pursed lips. With both hands, she grabbed Zana's head, shoving her onto the stiff rod, fucking her mouth merciless.

Zana took it all, choking as the rhythm of Magden's thrusts left her breathless. She pitched forward, her hand splitting her Reinè's gash with two fingers.

Magden cried out, and the hot, heady brew of her lust filled Zana's throat, her mouth, spilling from her lips. As soon as the sticky elixir ran over her tongue, Zana wanted to taste it deep inside her cunt. The excess slipped down her neck and ran in sweltering rivulets down her cleavage, staining the damp silk of her wedding gown.

Magden bent down, chasing it. Without ceremony, she tore the front of Zana's gown open, exposing her small bosom, tonguing the droplets of jism and natura from her Zephyris's flushed skin. Torn ribbons fell to the Apothecary floor.

Small spasms coursed over Zana's softer flesh and shivered deep between her legs. She felt the surge of strength through her Reinè's muscles, felt herself suddenly crushed tight, crushed breathless. Magden lifted her, carrying her. Zephyris instinct forced Zana's thighs wide, the hardness of her Reinè urging against her.

Crying out, she strained toward it, soaking Magden's scales, soaking her sex, both male and female. Her legs locked around her queen's waist, desperate as she moaned against her mouth.

Kissing her hard, the Primè Reinè stumbled. They collided with a glass cabinet, their weight shoving it against the wall. Although it didn't break, the alarming clink of bottles cast Zana's attention upward. Shelves jammed with fluted flasks, beakers, and bottles towered above them, their contents dismembered, blurred by a thick coating of dust and web.

Nearly sobbing, Zana spread herself. Her spine pressed against the glass cabinet, she balanced with one hand on the back of Magden's neck. The other slipped between the Reinè's legs, taking hold of her hard masculinity.

Magden's eyes were aflame, her breath panting. Zana guided her past the damp silk of her wedding dress, fingers yanking aside soaked panties. Slowly, she rubbed the Reinè's cock-tip against the soft petals of her cunt, slathering it with her wanton juices.

Moaning softly, Magden grabbed Zana's ass with both hands, shifting her into better position against the glass. The cabinet creaked but it didn't break. Holding her, watching her every move, Magden allowed Zana to guide her.

Smooth and tight, the Zephyris slid it in, even the first inch threatening to split her open. Writhing, she struggled to seduce Magden deeper into her pussy.

The Primè Reinè held her back.

Desperate, Zana kissed her hard, thrusting her tongue into Magden's mouth the way she wanted Magden's cock to thrust into her pussy. Moaning, whimpering, she struggled in vain.

The Reinè smiled, fingering the white silk of Zana's skirts.

"My wedding dress," the Zephyris whispered against her mouth. "Do you like it?"

Magden writhed, the resistance of Zana's slash taut against the tip of her cock. "It appears white is appropriate after all."

Zana blushed hot. She was nearly sobbing in frustration. Each time she moved closer, the Reinè held her away, barely keeping an inch of herself within. "Please, Magden..."

"You have to take yourself." Magden's luminous eyes met hers. "I won't take you. Not on your wedding night."

Panting, fraught with frustration, Zana gripped Magden's shoulders. Her eyes bright with excitement and fear, she met the gaze of her queen, and the Zephyris in her awoke in ardent lust.

Without pretense, she drove herself onto Magden's hard cock. A quivering whimper escaped her as smooth serpent-flesh penetrated her to the hilt.

Magden's eyes rolled back, her body spasming as Zana shafted herself. Long seconds passed while the Reinè fought for breath, for mastery of her chemical instincts. Zana rode her, crying out in ecstasy. Slowly, Magden mastered her lust, and then, inch by inch, she withdrew.

Zana couldn't stand it. Her gaze fell to her emerald scales, dying, peeling from her like withered parchment, and a different fear quaked inside her. *She doesn't want me... I'm too human.*

Her breath stopped as Magden shoved into her, splaying her wide. A hoarse cry tore from the Reinè's throat as she drove into Zana's pussy, slamming her against the cabinet, each thrust shoving her harder against the glass, beating it against the wall.

Bottles fell, shattering around them. Screaming, gasping, Zana held on as her Reinè split into her again and again, tearing the virginity from her cunt even as her claws tore the wedding gown into shreds.

Flasks hit the floor, smashing at their bare feet. Magden thrust harder and the cabinet shattered. Glass shards bit into Zana's thighs, her buttocks, the warm slide of blood mingling with come and sweat and natura from the Reinè's bestial rutting.

Zana clasped her tight, needing, wanting, even as Magden took her, filling her with her stiff cock. Each time she withdrew was like a bitter rejection. Zana clung to her as if she would never let go, her fingernails digging into Magden's back, drawing beads of emerald blood. Her body bucked, desperate to receive the seed of the Primè Reinè.

Was this how it had been between her mother and Magden's?

The Queen of the Nyth and her Zephyris concubine. Magden, her half-sister.

The thought sent a cascade of shivers through her.

Magden was lifting her again, carrying her to the altar. The smell of old viscera and medicine permeated the wood. Zana's pussy tightened in fear, and she felt the wetness of her blood and the juices of her frustration trickling down her thighs. Magden set her down on the edge, legs spread and dangling.

Without warning, she came into her hard, fucking Zana in long, deep strokes. Zana threw her head back, leaning on her palms to open her thighs wider. Her hips ached from the strength of Magden's fucking.

Nearing her crisis, the Reinè gasped, her breath coming ragged. Triumph flashed through Zana, and she bucked against her, sliding hard on Magden's phallus. An eager Zephyris, she wanted to taste her Reinè's come deep inside her pussy. Every thrust brought her closer.

Zana held her breath, on the edge of conquest.

Abruptly, Magden withdrew. Before Zana could protest, Magden grabbed her, rolling her face-down onto the table. Zana cried out in fear, her breasts crushed against the rotting wood. The smells of blood and come were thick in her nostrils, quickening in her belly, making her thighs quiver in hot anticipation.

The remnants of her wedding gown were pulled taut across her body, her thighs, the softness of her ass crushed by wet silk. She felt Magden's grip tighten, and the fabric tore like paper, ripping from her flushed body. Savage and soft, her Reinè's hands were on her, massaging her buttocks, spreading them wide. The hardness of Magden's cock prodded Zana's tight ass.

"No, Magden, don't!" *Goddess, yes!*

Magden split her wide, taking the virginity of her ass in one hard stroke. Taken breathless, Zana could not even scream. Her hands slapped against the table but found no purchase.

Gently, Magden pulled out of her. Tears on her lashes, Zana dared a glance back.

The Primè Reinè leaned over, her cobalt-blue scales

shimmering in the guttering light. Her mouth opened, and natura spilled from her lips. Thick and translucent, it coated her stiff member, running over the shaft, slicking the head like honey. Magden took herself in one hand, rubbing the tip against Zana's ass, smearing her chrism on Zana's aching hole.

The Zephyris moaned, the feel of the slippery liquid igniting her desire. Gripping the sides of the altar, she tilted her ass in the air.

Magden's hand clamped down on the back of her neck. A low hiss growled deep in her throat, and she entered Zana again. She meant only to thrust once, but the burning of her natura and the sweat of her Zephyris drew her in, pounding, her cock slapping relentless into Zana's tight hole, her breath gasping hoarse, her cries of rapture echoing into the darkness.

The storm raged, urging her on. Crimson wax spilled, running over the table like fresh blood.

Buffeted by her Reinè's bestial fucking, Zana took the first strokes submissively. Sudden pleasure burned through the pain, and she struggled to hands and knees. Magden's hands gripped her hips, rocking her back onto her unrelenting cock. Lurching forward, Zana jammed three fingers inside her needy hole. Moaning, panting like a whore, she pumped herself, her pussy, her ass quivering from the dual pounding—Magden's hard shaft sodomizing her from behind, her own fingers taking her from the front.

A shuddering cry escaped Magden, and she came in a convulsion, her hot seed spurting inside Zana's tight ass.

The Zephyris spasmed as her Primè Reinè drew back. Come and natura ran in rivulets down her thighs, over her glistening gash. Physically spent, her body bucked, still crying out for the release of orgasm. She rolled onto her back, legs splayed, the fusion of her pussy juice and Magden's seed staining the altar.

Relief stole her breath as Magden took her forcefully by the wrists, pinning her to the table. Her cries turned to groans of pleasure as the weight of her Reinè's body bore down on hers, and as Magden's hardness filled her needy pussy, she raked her nails down the Reinè's back, drawing lines of emerald blood.

The scent of their sex permeated the air, stifling the flickering candles. Deep at the back of her throat, Zana could taste Magden, but the essence of her grew more distant and foreign. Zana's blood continued its slow death.

Oblivious, Magden rutted atop her, her hands slipping from Zana's wrists. Lapis claws sheared from her fingertips, cutting slowly down the wood. Her thrusts came hard and fast, her cock slapping into Zana's pussy, splaying her asunder.

Delirious, Zana rode her queen, unable to recall the face of her betrothed. Gasps tore from her throat, her own orgasm threatening. Hot against her neck, Magden's moans turned deep and guttural. She raised herself, her eyes glowering a serpent gleam. A flash of lapis claws and the wood splintered around Zana's face, casting slivers about her.

Terrified, elated, Zana felt fused to her, mouth to mouth, cock to pussy, even as the Reinè invaded her human body with throbbing serpent-flesh. She remembered that night—the ritual, the storm, Magden's blade thrusting into her, penetrating her body, stealing her Nythian nature.

Once more, her gaze fell to her scales, withering a slow death. "Magden, please...get it over with. Kill me quickly."

Still buried deep within her Zephyris, the Primè Reinè drew back. Dark blue claws rose above Zana, casting a shadow on her face. She felt her pussy constrict in fear, bringing her to the brink of orgasm.

"Yes, Magden, cut me."

Thunder and lightning, lapis claws flashed through the night. Green blood struck the oak, fading quickly to red. Zana's screams lit the night, Magden's claws like needles of fire in her flesh, the stiffness of her cock ruthlessly fucking her.

A second scream, and Zana came in a torrent, her virginity spent against Magden's cock, spilling out onto the rotting wood. Her body jerked in the after-throes of sex and death, and her own natura poured forth in a slick tide, soaking them both. Like oil, it christened the table, mingling with the juices of their fucking.

Zana wracked, and the dying of her blood came quickly now, her Nythian essence spilling out on the altar. A sliver of human fright spiked her, and she knew fear of the creature above her. Like any prey held in thrall, she knew better than to struggle.

Magden trembled with the effort of holding back. Zana was no longer her Zephyris. Gathering herself, she moved to withdraw, her cock engorged, threatening to spill inside a human girl.

Defiance flashed in Zana's green eyes. Grabbing Magden by the wrist, she bucked, rolling her onto her back, pushing her down. Zana straddled her, one hand gripping the Reinè's swollen shaft, the other spreading the deprived lips of her cunt.

"Zana!"

With a shuddering breath, she drove herself hard onto Magden's stiff cock. Their screams rose in the night, the Reinè struggling to hold back, the dying Zephyris fulfilling her duty to the last breath.

And as the final vestiges of her Nythian blood died, as her scales withered and fell like ash, as the last of her night vision and her serpentine strength washed away in a flood of humanity, Zana forced herself onto Magden, driving the Nyth queen deeper and deeper into her aching pussy.

Her desire, her chemical need unbound, Magden grabbed Zana's hips and sheathed her cock again and again into the human girl until at last, her fangs bared and with a guttural groan, she came, spilling the sweltering heat of her seed into Zana's brazen cunt.

The human girl cried out in pleasure, in pain, riding out the aftershocks on the Reinè's masculinity. She could taste Magden's come at the back of her throat.

And then, Magden was lifting her, setting her down. She stumbled as her feet touched the stone floor. The Primè Reinè's come slicked down her thighs, and Zana ached all over from an ecstasy she would never again know.

Dazed, she looked to her wedding gown, shredded by Nyth

claws, stained with blood and *natura* and the come of her infidelity. And the dreadful weight of being human—only human—bore down upon her.

The Primè Reinè, Queen of the Nyth, stood before her, austere and terribly alien. Her slitted pupils dilated, and the musk of serpents shrouded her in a fearsome veil. "Go to your betrothed and wed him. Go to his bed with my seed still drying on your thighs."

Gathering the tatters of her wedding gown to her aching flesh, the human girl fled out into the storm.

Far-off, the morning temple bells rang, sounding the announcement of a wedding.

Contributors

Originally from a small town in coastal Mississippi, **T. K. Ashley** has since traveled and lived all over the world: from rural Vermont to medieval Russian cities, and from New Orleans to colonial Mexican towns. Her love of exploration applies as well to her love of reading, where her favorite authors range from Dostoevsky and Dickens to Robin McKinley, Joan D. Vinge, Jacqueline Carey and many, many others. She enjoys writing in the high fantasy, fairy tale, and historical fiction genres. She currently resides in Atlanta with her husband and two cats.

Kierstin Cherry was born in a tiny village in northern New England. Forced to attend an all-girl parochial school, she led the other girls in a revolt against the nuns and escaped into the wild. Raised by wolves and fairies, she found her calling as a semi-shy erotica writer and editor, and has recently graduated with her MFA in Writing Popular Fiction from Seton Hill University. Although Kierstin has a quirky, irreverent sense of humor, she is very serious about her work as an author and editor. She puts the romance back into necromancy with her erotic vampire stories, including "Graced," featured in the Lambda-nominated anthology *Women of the Bite* by Circlet Press ebooks and in print by Alyson Books.

Clarice Clique has had stories featured in many anthologies, including *Fantastic Erotica: The Best of Circlet Press 2008-2012*. Through her erotic writing she likes exploring relationships, the good the bad and the fantastically beautiful. Her BDSM novel, *Switch*, focuses on the intimate love and trust between a sub and dom. In her most recent novel, *The Kindness of Strangers*, she plays with the idea of what happens when couples experience the sexual intensity of a swingers weekend. When not writing, she's thinking about writing.

M. A. Earnshaw is a twenty-something from Yorkshire, England. She writes in her spare time and prefers not to think about her day job. Her sense of humour is generally best kept away from the public. She's single and looking forward to the day she can start collecting the pets who will eat her when she dies, and her hobbies include abusing the Twitter character limit and listening to an eclectic variety of music.

Michael M. Jones lives in Southwest Virginia, with too many books, a pride of cats, and a wife who reads his mind. His stories have appeared in numerous anthologies, such as Geek Love, Fantastic Erotica, and A Princess Bound. He is the editor of Like a Cunning Plan and Like Fortune's Fool, and also serves as Circlet's microfiction editor. Visit him at www.michaelmjones.com for more information.

Kara Owl writes about many things, both real and fantastic. She lives in Tallahassee, FL with four cats and a dog, and a very patient and understanding husband. You can visit her and learn more about her life at facebook.com/WriterKaraOwl.

Christina M. Parker has been writing and teaching about alternative relationships and spirituality for over 15 years. Her spiritual path focuses on sacred service and she self-identifies as a Priestess of Venus. A resident of Virginia, she lives in a haven of magic, mayhem, and geekery known as Shadowglen.

Jennifer Williams is an author, editor, and cat lady. Her most recent work is the anthology *Like a Sacred Desire: Tales of Sex Magick*, published by Circlet Press and featuring stories by Raven Kaldera, D. L. King, and David Sklar. She has also recently been published in the Lambda Literary Award-nominated collection *Women of the Bite*, edited by Cecilia Tan and *Vicious Verses and Reanimated Rhymes*, a collection of zombie poetry, edited by A. P. Fuchs. She is a Twilight Stories finalist and a proud fan girl/geek/comic book nerd.

Nadine Wilmot is: reader, scribbler, photographer, baker, faker, music-maker, semi-nomadic and insatiably curious. She has published short fiction in prior Circlet anthologies *Like A Cunning Plan* and *The Flesh Made Word*, as well as micro-fiction in *The Thackery T. Lambshead Cabinet of Curiosities*, edited by Ann and Jeff Vandermeer. She loves the world, even you. Especially you.

About the Publisher

Circlet Press has been publishing works of erotic fantasy and science fiction since 1992. Short story anthologies, novels, and online serials that celebrate the erotic imagination have filled the Circlet catalog for over 24 years. If you would like to stay up to date on what's new from Circlet Press, please join our newsletter list to receive monthly free reads or hop over to our Patreon to support our writers and receive access to the whole Circlet library.

Newsletter:http://www.circlet.com/contact-us/email-newsletter/

Patreon: https://www.patreon.com/circletpress

Like a Sacred Desire:
Tales of Sex Magick
Edited by Jennifer Williams

Volume 16 of the Erotic Fantasy & Science Fiction Selections series. The latest erotic fantasy anthology from Circlet Press explores sex magick and the sacred aspect of sex in seven all-new stories where sex is a sacrament, a gateway to spiritual healing and higher consciousness. Authors including Raven Kaldera, D.L. King, Angela Caperton, and more invite readers on a journey both sensual and spiritual, where nothing is quite what it seems.

Fantastic Erotica:
The Best of Circlet Press 2008-2012
Edited by Cecilia Tan & Bethany Zaiatz

To celebrate the 20th Anniversary of Circlet Press, Fantastic Erotica presents the very best erotic science fiction and fantasy short stories published by Circlet in the past five years. Chosen by popular vote by the readership from among all the stories published by Circlet from 2008 to the present, these favorites are the cream of the crop.

Circlet
Press

Like a Cunning Plan:
Erotic Trickster Tales
Edited by Michael M. Jones

Volume 25 of the Erotic Fantasy & Science Fiction Selections series. Everyone loves a trickster. Armed with a clever smile and a quick wit, they act as agents of change, leaving chaos and confused victims in their wake. In Like A Cunning Plan, gods and mortals alike interact in sexy, playful, sensual ways, and it's anyone's guess as to who comes out on top. Featuring stories by Nica Berry, N. Violett, Nadine Wilmot, Elizabeth Schecter, Gayle C. Straun, Kaysee Renee Robichaud, and Sunny Moraine, these erotic fantasies are sure to surprise and satisfy.

Like a God's Kiss:
Erotic Mythological Tales
Edited by Cecilia Tan & Jennifer Levine

Volume 8 of the Erotic Fantasy & Science Fiction Selections series. Like a God's Kiss combines the epic and the erotic, the mythological and the real, to culminate in seven engaging and steamy stories. With protagonists ranging from heroic Hercules to arrogant Arachne and plots ranging from the well-known to the never-before-seen, readers will discover all new aspects about their favorite mythological characters, and will be introduced to a few new ones as well.

www.ingramcontent.com/pod-product-compliance
Lightning Source LLC
Chambersburg PA
CBHW060233180626
46813CB00007B/3061